THE IRISH MARTYR

THE RICHARD SULLIVAN PRIZE IN SHORT FICTION

Editors
William O'Rourke and Valerie Sayers

THE IRISH MARTYR

RUSSELL WORKING

UNIVERSITY OF NOTRE DAME PRESS

NOTRE DAME, INDIANA

Library of Congress Cataloging in-Publication Data

Working, Russell, 1959–
The Irish martyr / Russell Working.
p. cm. — (The Richard Sullivan prize in short fiction)
ISBN-13: 978-0-268-04408-4 (pbk. : alk. paper)
ISBN-10: 0-268-04408-2 (pbk. : alk. paper)
I. Title.   II. Series.
PS3573.06926175   2006
813'.54—dc22
2005035137

To Nonna, Seryoga, and Lyova

CONTENTS

ACKNOWLEDGMENTS

"The Irish Martyr" first appeared in *Zoetrope: All-Story,* "Halloween, Via Dolorosa" in *The Paris Review,* "Perjury" in *TriQuarterly Review,* "The World in the First Year of the Wire" in *Mississippi Mud,* "Inmates" in *Notre Dame Review,* "Help" in *The Atlantic Monthly,* and "Dear Leader" in *Kyoto Journal.*

In conceiving the mother's background story in "The Irish Martyr," I was indebted to the Middle East Media Research Institute for its January 2002 translation of a letter to the *Akhbar Al-Yaum* newspaper, titled "The Egyptian Wife's Tale."

A basement full of 1917 bound volumes of the Grants Pass, Oregon, *Rogue River Courier* (now the *Daily Courier*) provided a number of quotes (and inspired some fictional riffs) in "The World in the First Year of the Wire."

I have interlarded "Dear Leader" with press releases from the Korean News Service. The agency did indeed report on the land realignment project in North Phyongan Province, though I have trimmed here and there and added boilerplate from other North Korean propaganda. I have left unaltered a press release on the miraculous return of white herons to Mangyongdae on the anniversary of Kim Il-Sung's death.

Robert Jay Lifton's *Thought Reform and the Psychology of Totalism: A Study of "Brainwashing" in China* (New York: Norton, 1961) proved invaluable in writing "Inmates."

I am grateful for a fellowship at Yaddo that allowed me to finish several of these stories.

Michael Ray, Reginald Gibbons, Cortlan Bennett, Rick Moody, Ken Rodgers, James Linville, and Cullen Murphy offered invaluable suggestions on various stories. I am indebted to Ann Aydelotte for her insights and graceful touch in editing this book, and for her careful fact-checking, right down to the Italian lyrics of the opera I quote. My wife, Nonna, undertook the thankless task of typing several published stories into the computer. She also encouraged me to compile and submit this collection in the first place, offered wise insights, and kept me from stumbling in my depiction of Russia, her former homeland, and once my home, too.

Finally, I never would have written "Dear Leader" had not a North Korean refugee and the Chinese peasant who bought her as his wife welcomed me into their home and allowed me to interview them in the spring of 2000. They endangered themselves in order to tell their story to a foreign journalist. This is a work of fiction, but I nonetheless hope my audacity in conceiving lives very different from mine does justice to them and others who have fled the Democratic People's Republic of Korea. I hope the two of them have found happiness together. I hope they are safe.

THE IRISH MARTYR

NADIA FIRST SAW THE FOREIGNER ON HER THIRD DAY IN AL-ARISH, as she and Ghaada went to swim. The Awar girls came here with their parents every August—just the four of them, now that their older sister was married and their brother remained in Cairo running a small chain of pizza parlors that Papa owned—but Nadia had never seen this stranger, or, for that matter, any foreigner in this Mediterranean town, with its litter-blown beaches and donkeys hauling carts of olives or apricots. He was wiry and ruddy, with angular limbs and a hollow where his sternum met his throat. The girls passed him as he returned from a swim. He was dripping wet and wearing gym shorts, nothing more, and although his torso was almost hairless and milky in color, sunburn and a grotesque pox of freckles stained his face and forearms. He had not shaved that morning. He was blue-eyed and handsome, or would have been without the freckles. He stared at the sisters, surprised, it seemed, to see young women heading out to swim while wearing long dresses and Islamic head scarves. At the last instant before he passed, he winked. Nadia looked away. Ghaada suffocated her giggles.

They waded into the shallow waves, as salty as bouillon, and their dresses billowed in the spume, so that someone swimming under the roiling surface could have seen the teal and purple of their bathing suits. "He likes you," Ghaada said, and she gathered her garments around her and submerged before Nadia could answer. At fourteen—two years younger than Nadia—Ghaada had already joined the legions of conservative girls who had concluded that there was no point in keeping one's weight down when even the most general outlines of one's body were hidden from the eyes of men, so they ate with the appetites of field hands and paraded the streets like blimps in raincoats. For Nadia, however, baklava and Wagon Wheels did not provide the escape they did Ghaada, and so she had grown up willowy, with a figure she would admire in the bathroom mirror as she emerged from the shower: she would let the towel slip away, revealing the volumes of her body, the breasts, the shapely belly with its ant-like trail of hair, the spiral of a navel, the shorn triangle where her legs met. Even on the streets in her formless dresses, she felt men's eyes when the wind blew and the fabric clung to her.

When Ghaada surfaced, Nadia splashed her. "You're an idiot. He's obviously an infidel."

"So? I saw how he looked at you. I wonder what he's doing here."

"He's probably one of those crazy cyclists heading from Istanbul to Cairo. Or maybe he was traveling to Sharm el-Sheikh, and he got on the wrong bus. Anyway, he'll leave soon, God willing. What's there to do in Arish?"

But the stranger did not seem to be headed anywhere. He settled on the patio on the beachside of his cottage, a flat-roofed stucco "villa," as they were advertised, that sat beside an identical one the Awars were renting. A walkway half a meter wide separated the buildings. By the time the girls returned from their swim, the foreigner had pulled on a T-shirt that read, in English, "H-Block Martyrs"—the fabric a faded green that reassumed its original color below his waistband, where it adhered to his swimsuit. He sprawled in a lawn chair thumbing through a copy of the *Middle East Times* and drinking a bottle of Stella beer, even at this hour, not yet one in the afternoon. As they washed their feet at the saltwater tap, Nadia sneaked another look. The man was watching her, and her gaze fell to a crack in the concrete that channeled the runoff into a hydra-headed delta on the sand. Was he still looking? She dared not check. Such a man was probably used to eyeing topless blondes shivering on the wind-swept beaches of Europe, and Nadia imagined that he could discern things about her in her wet garments.

Papa—a stout man, prematurely elderly at fifty-three, with wood-colored teeth that had rotted to fangs, like a shark's—stepped out for a smoke and noticed the foreigner. "Hello," the stranger said in Arabic, but

Papa did not understand the man's pronunciation. He glowered, and the stranger sat up a little, alert. Then it dawned on him that Papa was directing his lightning bolts of wrath at the bottle, which now stood on a low wall, and, shaking his head, the stranger took the bottle indoors. Moments later he returned carrying a coffee mug topped off with froth, as if porcelain disguised his sin in the eyes of the Omniscient One, Most Beneficent, Most Merciful.

— By the time the girls had changed, Papa was back in the biggest bedroom complaining to Mama. Fully dressed, she lay atop the bedclothes clutching a windup alarm clock with double brass hemispheres on top, registering its hypertensive ticktock like the pulse of a mechanical hummingbird. The shutters were closed, and a ceiling fan stirred the indolent flies that patrolled the honeycombed volumes of space in redundant sorties.

"Who does he think he is, strolling around practically naked out there, leering at good Muslim girls?" he demanded, as if Mama had been complicit in the foreigner's lechery.

Mama drew a breath as if to speak, but did not.

"Look at him, guzzling beer in front of the girls. And at this hour. That's what these infidels are like. I've warned you and the girls about foreigners, and you laughed at me. And now you all can finally see with your own eyes. A man like that would gladly take advantage of you." This last statement he directed toward the living room, where the girls stood, afraid to sit or retreat to their own room. "You can see the kind of people they are. Nakedness, drunkenness, lechery."

Finally, Mama's eyes turned to him with such loathing that an attentive person would take a hint and leave her alone. "Why don't you go beat him up, then?"

He did not notice the sarcasm. "If he keeps it up, I might do it, God willing. But I'll tell you something: The girls are not going out on the beach while he's there."

"Papa, we can't stay indoors all day in the summer," Nadia said. "It's forty-three degrees today."

"You've got better things to do, anyway. Go listen to a tape and improve your mind."

■ The girls sat in their room—on the west side of the house, across the walkway from the foreigner's place—and listened to the preacher's warnings about women, who were weak by nature and, were it not for the teachings of the Prophet—God's blessing and peace be upon him—and the supervision of their fathers and husbands, would give in to the sins of gossip or flirtation or jangling their finery under their robes, generation upon generation, always the same. For when the Prophet went to hell, did he not see more women there than men? The preacher illustrated the sermon with an incident he had witnessed in Giza: a young hussy boarding a bus wearing a black dress that bared her forearms and her legs from the knees down—so exposed was she that one gust of the dun western wind had been sufficient to reveal certain garments to those boarding behind her, and when the good men and women of the bus reproved her and said there were places where people knew how to deal with the likes of her—through stonings, honor killings, cutting off noses, and such—this defiant young harlot was reduced to tears and retorted that she was an Egyptian citizen and they had no right to tell her she should take the veil if she did not elect to. But who knows? Perhaps these good people had planted the seeds of repentance that would save her from the unquenchable fires of hell, God willing, for the Almighty was Oft Forgiving and Most Merciful. This woman interested Nadia, but the preacher moved on to a denunciation of similar transgressors, such as a tramp who stood in the doorway of her apartment openly talking with a male clerk from the Energy Ministry who had come to collect the electric bill, or the woman who did not bother to put on her head scarf, but merely a baseball cap, when she went out to hang the laundry from the balcony of the mud-brick apartment where she lived, oblivious, apparently, to the longing eyes of teenage boys nearby or to the possibility that she might distract even, say, a devout man who might happen to be sitting at a window across the courtyard, tearing him away from his reflection on God's Holy Book—for are we not all human and corruptible if we do not exercise vigilance?

The tape went on for a long time. Nadia peeked through a crack between the drawn curtains and glimpsed, in the space between the cottages, the foreigner's leg hanging over the wall. Sometimes his hand—holding his cup, a cigarette, or both—rested on the leg. "I'll tell Papa you're looking," Ghaada said, but the threat was entirely idle: the consequences would have been so dire—a firestorm of wrath that could end in the beating of both girls—that it could not be taken seriously.

The afternoon grew hotter, but even without the presence of a foreigner, another swim would have been out of the question, for there was dinner to prepare, and Mama could not go to the market because visible waves of nausea were smutting her vision. The girls walked up the road by the flat-roofed stucco houses. Most women they saw wore the *hijab*, like Nadia and Ghaada, but a few saintly sisters ghosted by in black chadors, their eyes flitting to take in the portion of the world allotted to them, as if through a slot in a steel door. Two Coptic girls, in jeans and T-shirts that read "Limassol Wine Festival 2002" and "All the Cats of Cyprus," strolled along chattering as they licked ice-cream cones. Farther on, a group of teenage boys in shorts and T-shirts and floppy beach hats were wrestling with each other on the sidewalk, but they stopped when the Awar sisters approached.

Near the mosque were a number of bearded Islamists, wearing white skullcaps and short-sleeved outfits like nightshirts, through which the silhouettes of their legs and their underwear could be discerned. Scriptures wailed from the loudspeaker in the minaret, and a drowsy policeman, dressed in a red beret and white uniform and black boots, guarded an automated teller machine with his Kalashnikov slung over his shoulder. A new photo lab had opened since the Awars were last in al-Arish, and the owner was crouching inside the display window, adjusting his portraits of newlyweds in gilded frames. But his own handiwork was dwarfed by posters of the gold-domed Noble Sanctuary, of the decapitated head of a martyr—just the head: his eyes smudged, his beard singed—lying in a supermarket amid a shambles of arms and legs and crushed cantaloupes and grapes and strollers. According to a caption, he had blasted himself straight through the gates of Paradise, God willing, while sending several infant Zionists and their mothers and a reserve soldier to hell. There was also a poster of a dead boy of eight or ten years lying in a coffin draped in a Palestinian flag, but when Nadia stopped to study it, Ghaada said, "Let's go. I can't stand this."

Along the market street the girls picked through the shops and side stalls selling dates, peanuts, live chickens in cages, Orbit gum, Crest toothpaste, Coca-Cola, packages of Abu Ammar potato chips decorated with a cartoon of President Arafat's gaping bespectacled face, Iranian soaps of a brand called Barf. When Ghaada had come home recently with a bottle of Barf dishwashing detergent, Mama laughed for the first time since before the day in February when they found her unconscious on the kitchen floor with an empty bottle of sleeping tablets beside her. "I don't know what this word means in Farsi," she said, "but in English it's what the cat keeps doing behind Papa's chair." Sides of beef and goat hung out in front of the butcher shops in the Sinai heat, but their color was bad. Eventually the sisters found some fresh mutton. By the time they returned, the boys were gone.

— That night after bedtime, Nadia peeked once again at the foreigner's place. His window was opposite the girls', and his lights were on. The curtains were of tulle, flimsy and translucent, and Nadia could see into the room where he was pacing about in blue shorts and his Martyrs T-shirt, gnawing on a drumstick. The remainder of his dinner—the carcass of a chicken, an olive salad, some pita, a smear of hummus—was served on paper plates laid out on a tablecloth made of a copy of *Al-Ahram*. "What are you doing?" Ghaada said.

Nadia shushed her with a scowl. For a time the foreigner was out of view. Then he returned and swept the remains and the newspaper into the trash and wiped down the table with a rag. Vanishing again, he left only his shadow on the wall, his arms working at something; then he came back drying his hands on his shorts. From a shelf nearby, he grabbed what looked like a billiard case and opened it on the table. He unpacked some steel rods and pipes and a pencil box and the padded end of a crutch, all of them black. With a glance at his watch, he fit them together rapidly, biting his lip. "Can you see him?" Ghaada whispered. He screwed the pad onto a rod and fitted that to the pencil box. A thin pipe was attached to the other end. It hit Nadia that he was assembling a rifle—a sleek, lightweight weapon, nothing like the bulky Kalashnikovs shouldered by the police. He screwed on a silencer and rechecked his watch. Satisfied, he set the rifle on its mounts—an inverse V, with an I under the butt—and knelt behind the table, aiming in the direction of the beach. He peered through the scope and fingered the trigger.

"Pow," he said. Nadia could read his lips through the windows. "Pow."

Then he disassembled the rifle and cleaned it with rags and a long, thin brush.

"What's he doing?" Ghaada said.

"Nothing."

"I want to look."

"Hush. You can't."

"You're looking."

"He just put a rifle together."

Ghaada shoved her way to the window. The man sensed something and looked toward them, and the girls ducked.

After they deemed it safe to speak, Ghaada whispered, "We should tell Papa."

"Tell him what? That we were spying on a man in his room? You know what he'll do to us."

"Maybe he's going to kill somebody."

"Why would a foreigner come to Egypt to kill somebody?"

■ When the stranger sprawled out on his patio a second day, the girls were again forbidden to swim. In the morning, Papa alone ambled out, wearing trunks and a singlet, his skinny legs exposed, and belly-flopped into the lukewarm sea. Meanwhile, Nadia and Ghaada sat indoors, bored and quarrelsome, until Mama sent them to get some cayenne candies. The time in al-Arish was not all vacation for Papa; he was setting up another franchise here, so he left for the afternoon, and Mama remained in her room, sometimes lying facedown on the bed, sometimes sitting in a rocking chair holding the clock. Nadia sat with her and asked about the stories she already knew but which Mama used to like to recount. Once Grandpa, for example, had taken the entire family to Aswan when he was consulted on an important technical question concerning the dam. He was an engineer and a tender man, and his eyes always followed Grandma wherever she was in the room, even after she was old and liver-spotted, and she smiled modestly as if not wishing to flaunt her good fortune. Uncle Basel, who as a boy would chase Mama outside with the scarabs he found, ended up studying in Paris and stole a small marker that read "Jim Morrison" from Père Lachaise graveyard ("He wanted an unmarked grave: I read it somewhere," Uncle Basel had said), but then, in a fit of guilt, he tried to return it and was arrested. And later, when Mama was in university, a professor had told her that someday she would be interpreting for Egypt at the United Nations or in Washington or Sydney, her English was that good—but that was before she found a job at the translation service and met Papa, who needed help corresponding with an American corporation. Only after their wedding did he tell her, "You obviously were not granted beauty, and you must admit that makeup does not improve your face. Be content with my accepting you as you are, with your face and your weight. I want you as God created you, with no artificial beautification. And you must terminate all contact with your workplace. You needn't submit your resignation; just quit showing up, without an explanation. After fifteen days they'll fire you, in accordance with the law. After all, who needs them?" Nadia also knew that all the relatives despised Papa and had urged Mama to leave her husband, but for some reason, she had never found the courage to do this.

Today, however, she did not wish to talk. "I don't want to think about it. I just want to rest."

"Mama, stop looking at that." Nadia snatched the clock and set it aside.

"Time goes more slowly when you're aware of it. You savor it."

"It's not healthy. Tell me about that cruise to Lebanon when you were little."

But Mama picked up the clock again and said only, "Twenty-eight years."

This was the amount of time she had been married to Papa.

— When the stranger sat outside on the third straight day, Papa decided to speak to him. Never mind the pretense that he did not comprehend Arabic: usually these foreigners feigned ignorance, but you could see in their eyes that they understood. The girls sat on the couch by the open double doors in the living room, where they could crane and see what was going on.

"What are you up to in Arish?" Papa asked. "It's a long way from Giza and Luxor. Are you a spy?"

The foreigner raised his hands apologetically and replied in English. Nadia caught the words "sorry" and "Arabic." Papa had never permitted the girls to go to school, but they had learned to read at home; Mama also taught them English, and the exotic alphabet and words had excited Nadia, with their redolence of another world, of glass buildings and buttressed cathedrals and immobile Beefeaters and black taxicabs crowding the snowy pavement and girls who sauntered the streets in tight jeans with their navels exposed, but Nadia found it difficult to master the language without the discipline of school.

Papa continued as if the man understood. "Or maybe you're just a libertine. You shouldn't drink in public. It's a disgrace. You want to go to hell, it's your choice, but don't set a filthy example for my daughters. We come to the beach and they're cooped up in the stuffy house all week because of your public drunkenness. Besides, you shouldn't stare at them. I know what's on your mind when you leer at Nadia that way."

The foreigner pulled out a packet of Dunhills and shook one out at Papa. Flustered, Papa accepted. He lit his cigarette, then ignited the foreigner's.

"Well, that's all I had to say. No offense, eh? Just a few words of advice. Ah, I used to smoke Dunhills, but I gave them up. The good thing about smoking Cleopatras is you cut back. They taste so awful, I'm down to half a pack a day. That should add a few years to my life, God willing. You understand me?"

The stranger nodded on cue. It was obvious he did not.

"You know, smoke?" Papa puffed in an exaggerated manner, having suddenly taken it upon himself to teach an infidel the language of God. "Too bad my wife can't come out. She used to speak English quite well, and I'm starting to think you're an Englishman, eh? You seem to like our view. The sea? Ocean? Big water? It's lovely here, isn't it? Tell other foreigners to come, spend money. You are welcome to Egypt. But you must behave. If you must drink, keep it indoors. And the women: stick with your own kind. Our women are the most beautiful on earth, and once they marry they are lionesses in bed because they have been denied satisfaction so long, but they're not for you. You don't understand a word of what I'm saying, do you? Are you going to be here long? Long time? Many nights? Sleep?" He folded his hands under his cheek. The stranger laughed at Papa's antics, and Papa himself could not help chuckling. "Because if you are, I should find someone to interpret for me. You think I'm joking. This is serious."

━ That night, Papa telephoned the imam to seek help. "The situation is rather awkward," he explained. "I'm not saying he's a bad fellow. I just need someone to tell him there are standards of conduct when you live next door to a good Muslim family." Within an hour a Mercedes taxicab clattered up in a cloud of smoke and two men came to the door. They were a mismatched pair: Ibrahim, a garrulous young Palestinian cabdriver who nursed a hatred for the Israelis who had bulldozed his parents' house in Rafah, was clean-shaven and wore sneakers and jeans and a Chicago Bulls T-shirt, while his partner, who never stated his name, was a fat, gloomy, bearded man in a brown suit and a black-and-white kaffiyeh. When the visitors entered, the girls retreated to their room and listened through the vent in the door.

"I'm sorry about the problems you've been having," Ibrahim said. "We have already spoken to your neighbor, and he was mortified to learn he has offended you. He extends his apologies to you and your elder daughter, whose chaste beauty he admits he admired." (Nadia's heart was racing. Ghaada elbowed her.) "Things are different in Ireland. Infidels. You understand. But listen to me: this guy is with us. He has work to do, God willing. You could have blown everything, blabbing around like that. Thank God, the imam happened to call me because I speak English. I'm not blaming you. You didn't know. I'm just saying you must drop this. Discuss him with no one. Forget he exists, you and your family. We're deadly serious."

"I'm sorry, I had no idea. I would never tell a soul. I'm of course thrilled that he wishes to join the struggle—" Papa hesitated, perhaps uncertain what struggle they were talking about, though logic suggested the one against the Zionist entity. He pressed on: "If he needs help, I have relatives in Gaza who can—"

"Listen. If you breathe a word to anyone, we'll cut your throat like a sheep. Is that clear?"

"But I wouldn't—there's no need—" Papa faltered.

"Tell your family. It goes for all of you. Say nothing. To no one. Here or in Cairo. Ever. Till the day that you die. Forget you ever saw him."

That night a light through the window woke Nadia, and she thought, He's awake. Ghaada was snoring, and Nadia checked her alarm clock: two thirteen a.m. She lay there remembering Ibrahim's words, how the foreigner had admired her "chaste beauty"—how, when confronted with a report of Papa's affront, he had extended his apologies like a gentleman. She wished she could apologize in turn for her father's boorishness. Nadia knelt on her bed and peeked through the curtains. The Irishman had just returned from a swim, and, to her astonishment, he slipped off his trunks and stood there naked, toweling himself. He had not removed the hair of his body, and it was of a darker red than the hair of his head. After tossing the towel aside, he absently tugged on his penis. Something prickled between her legs. She knew it was iniquitous to spy on a naked man in his cottage, but she could not tear herself away. The foreigner vanished for a time, then returned, fully dressed, with his backpack and rifle case, which he propped against the table. Something popped in the walls, and Nadia started and lay down. Just the house contracting. She dared not look out the window again. Deep inside something was ticking, and as she lay there, she brought the Irishman into her room. In this fantasy, Ghaada was elsewhere, back home in Cairo, away at a friend's. Nadia warned him, "Get out of here or I'll scream. My Papa will kill you," but the Irishman pressed his lips to hers. She would be naked under the sheets, and his hands would touch her, starting with her shoulders. He smoothed the gooseflesh of her breasts, then moved down to her abdomen, lingering on her lower belly, slipping to the prickly, shaven salient. Then his fingers moved within. "It's true: you're a lioness," he whispered. Something pulsed deep inside her and caused her to gasp for breath. Sweat soaked her nightgown. Gradually the ecstasy subsided into remorse. "Ghaada?" she whispered. Asleep. Nadia did not understand what had happened, but maybe it helped you have a baby, if a man was with you. She wished there was somebody she could consult—Mama, her older sister, somebody—but she knew she could never speak a word about it. Nothing. To no one. Ever. Till the day that you die.

Breathe a word to anyone, we'll cut your throat like a sheep.

■ The next morning, the Irishman was gone, but his Martyrs T-shirt lay out on the chair on the patio. When there was no sign of him by noon, Papa let the girls go swimming again. "I doubt we'll be seeing much of him after Ibrahim told him off for me," Papa said. "He said this Irishman was quite ashamed of himself. You see, even unbelievers can have a conscience when confronted by decency." Nadia stared, and Papa flushed. "Don't tell anyone about him, by the way," he added. "He's doing some important work. Top-secret." Over time, the T-shirt blew onto the concrete, flapped like a stingray to a corner of the patio, and took refuge amid the broken glass and potato chip wrappers. Nadia kept hoping the Irishman would return for it.

But on Sunday, Papa came home waving a newspaper and announced, "Listen, girls. I've found our foreigner." He read aloud a story on page three. It seemed there had been a great victory in the Occupied Territories. A sniper, sitting on a hill near a Jewish settlement, had staked out the Zionist monkeys and pigs arriving for an evening school carnival and, in rapid succession, picked off three parents, six children, and two soldiers while the Israelis scrambled to figure out where the shooting was coming from. Obviously, he was a professional: he had popped off exactly eleven rounds, one for each enemy, then laid down his rifle and walked away. Every one of his so-called victims had died, except for one Zionist kindergartner who was rendered "a vegetable." Papa considered this, nodded once, then read on. The gunman nearly escaped, but the thrice-accursed Israelis, with their night-vision goggles, had found him fleeing and gunned him down. He was carrying an Australian passport, but the Zionists were investigating the possibility that he was connected to ("Get this," Papa said) the Irish Republican Army.

"An Irishman! I'm sure it's our neighbor. He was a little rough around the edges, but a decent young man nonetheless. Maybe he converted to Islam in the end, God willing. If so, today he's in paradise with seventy-two virgins."

That day, Nadia retrieved the T-shirt—which still smelled of a man—and when the Awars left al-Arish she brought it with her. She often daydreamed about the Irishman, but at night she would sometimes start awake, wondering what had become of the kindergartner, who lay in a hospital somewhere, unseeing, never thinking, day and night. She kept the shirt for three years, until after her wedding to Taisir, her father's accountant. But Taisir resented the stories Papa whispered about this Irish martyr. How did they know he had converted? Were his head and body hair shaven when he died? Was he carrying prayer beads, a Koran? He was probably just a mercenary. It was a diabolical lie to suggest that an infidel could be a martyr; the time had come for Nadia to throw away the shirt.

Taisir also made her toss out other frivolous possessions: letters from girl-friends, jewelry that tempted her to cupidity, an English-language text-book, a map of London from her mother. He forbade her to work, but that was not really an issue, because she could not get a job in the first place without an education. Nadia found ways to pass the time at home. Whenever her husband left for work, she turned the clock to face the wall, and she disciplined herself not to look at it until he returned. She did not wish to become like her mother.

HALLOWEEN, VIA DOLOROSA

THOUGH IT WAS DARK ON THE ROAD WHERE THE FOXES PARKED AND you tried to keep from stepping in the puddles of icy mud when you looked up at the stars, Ashland's North Main Street was brightly lighted and decorated with lamps and paper jack-o'-lanterns in the windows, and the street was closed off for Halloween with flashing barricades and crowded from one end to the other: from the tightly packed mob around the bandstand where a group was pounding out music and jumping sometimes with their guitars, to the end of the road near Gepetto's, where the crowd thinned out and everyone stopped and stood, puzzled and bemused, before turning back to walk again. They looked at each other, and now at this end of the street it seemed funny and innocent. Some of them were really good. A giant in a blue gown was lurching through the crowd, and small men held sticks attached to each arm. They made the giant wave. The pirate Jesse held his father's hand.

"Look!"

"Shakespeare," Fox said.

Fox was a monster. He had a Gila monster's head, with green fur on the pate and down the back of the neck, and he wore a coat and jeans and tennis shoes. He was smoking a cigar, stuck in a hole in the mask's gullet, and when he puffed, smoke came out of his eyes. People laughed and pointed at Fox. "Look at that guy," a witch said. "I love you." Fox was walking, and he bumped into her.

He said something, and she went on.

"You bumped her," said Jesse.

Fox mumbled something.

"What?"

He bent over by Jesse's ear. "I can't see out of this thing. The eye slits are too small. Would you help steer your old man? I'll take it off in a minute."

"Okay, Dad."

"Do you like this?"

"Yeah."

"Is it scary, kid?"

"No. A little bit."

"Good. A little scary is fun, isn't it?"

"Yeah."

"Let's head back down the street."

They went toward the noise.

Nuns were the most common, and, after them, buxom women in shiny red low-cut dresses with fringe around the edges. Richard Nixon was popular, too. Some nuns wore real habits and rosaries and might have been nuns for all you could tell except that one of them was saying, "Son of a bitch," as she swished past. The Foxes were Lutheran, not Roman Catholic. There was no such thing as Lutheran nuns.

Fox was hot, and the mask full of smoke, making his eyes water. He blinked. His breath condensed on the plastic and ran in cold rivulets into his collar. He gritted the cigar in his teeth so it would not touch the plastic and melt it.

An eight-legged Chinese dragon danced past. It trotted in step, weaving its way through the crowd, and headed straight for Fox, until Jesse realized his father would be trampled and pulled him hard to the left and the dragon went on by. Its eyes were lit up.

"Boy, that startled me," Fox said. "Where did that come from? I ought to take this off so I can see. Maybe one more trip down the street to show off. I've got one more cigar. Then I need to see, too."

Fox pulled off his mask and lit another cigar. His hair was messy and damp, and he grinned and winked at Jesse. He put the mask back on. He could not find the mouth hole, and he nearly stuck the cigar in his eye.

"Everybody's staring at you, Dad."

"They envy my costume. Kmart special."

Fox managed to get the cigar in the hole of the mask, and he puffed away. His eyes smoked, and some girls laughed and said, "Cool."

A cowboy came by with his horse attached around his midriff. He walked on his own feet, and the horse's legs dangled. He fired a cap gun in the air.

"Dad!"

"Yep."

Then a giant furry blond figure appeared, his head dark against a globe of light around a streetlamp, and Jesse stopped flat. The creature squatted beside the boy. He growled, "The Force be with you."

Fox snarled at him and the creature rose and growled, hands on his hips. Then he strode on. He had tennis shoes instead of furry padded feet.

"He's a good guy, Dad."

"I know. Gorillas are always good guys."

"It wasn't a gorilla. It was Chewbacca from *Star Wars*."

"No kidding?" Fox looked back over his shoulder. "I couldn't tell."

"You growled at him."

"It was a friendly growl."

Jesse led his father along past a six-pack of beer trotting down the road. The cans were laughing. "We'd never make it through the door," a can hollered back at someone.

The nuns were everywhere. One nun knelt in the street, holding up a stick with a doll on the end. The doll was covered with ketchup, which dripped down the stick onto her hands. She cried out in a quavery voice, "Sinners! You're on the road to hell. Stop the slaughter of the innocents."

A crowd stood in a circle around her, laughing. Ronald Reagan poured beer on her and made the sign of the cross.

"The name of the Father and the Son and the Holy Ghost," President Reagan said.

The crowd howled.

"What are they doing, Dad?"

"What?" Fox looked around. He tilted his head back so he could see through the nostrils. He gripped Jesse's hand tight and said, "Let's walk on," and he shoved his way through the crowd, dragging his son by the hand. They bumped into a man in a dress, who said "Ooo!" Fox said, "We don't need to look at them."

"What were they doing?"

"Just being stupid."

"Were they taking the Lord's name in vain?"

"Yes."

Satan walked past in a red skintight suit. A pentacle was drawn on his forehead, and one of his arms was artificial, with a shiny metal hook on the end. Jesse was going to say something about the arm to his father when he realized it was a real prosthesis. Fox was chewing the end of his cigar and looking the other way. Jesse squeezed his father's hand.

They were close to the band now, and the crowd made a noise, and through a gap Jesse saw Jesus. Jesus wore only a loincloth; he trudged along carrying a hollow plywood cross. A crown of thorns encircled his head, and stripes from a scourging were painted on his body. Jesse felt sick.

"Dad," he said. "Jesus."

Fox was puffing rapidly on the stub of his cigar; it was getting too short to be safe, and it might melt the plastic. He took a few final draws, then dropped the cigar on the pavement and ground it out under his sole. He removed the mask and said, "Ah. Now I can breathe."

"Dad," said Jesse. "A man dressed as Jesus."

Fox looked, and his face hardened. The man Jesus was grinning, and he bellowed, "*Eloi, Eloi, lama sabachthani.*" Some people laughed, but an old man standing near the Foxes told a woman dressed as Charlie Chaplin, "I can't believe it. I bloody cannot believe it."

"Let's get out of here," Fox said.

They walked up the street, and Jesse held his father's trembling hand. Fox wore his mask like a hat, and his face showed below the eyebrows. A couple of drunk college students staggered by, and one of them pointed at Fox and said, "Look at that one. He's fucking ugly."

Jesse started to cry. The other college boy said, "Now look what you've done," as they weaved away.

It was a long walk to the car, and Fox carried Jesse on his back. On the way they approached a small trailer parked in a lot full of weeds up past the railroad tracks, and a light was on, glowing through the yellow curtains and filmy broken window that was patched with duct tape. Jesse wiped his cheeks on his father's shoulders and thought, If only we make it that far. If we pass the window with the light on and the barking dog, we'll stay alive. If we make it to the car. Fox's pace was plodding, and Jesse thought, If he would run. If I stay awake that far.

The dog chained to an orange tree was barking, and it paced under the canopy of slick oily leaves and howled. The chain was long enough so that the dog could reach Jesse if it tried, but a python was coiled around the dog's legs and torso. You should stay away from the dog, Jesse knew, but the snake was deadly. The snake left the dog and slithered across the grass at him. Jesse thought, A weapon, and there was a machete in his hand. He beheaded the snake. The head was snapping on the ground, and Jesse leaped out of the way of the fangs. Then the Devil said to him, "Pick it up."

Fox carried him away and brought him inside the trailer. Jesse said, "Why are we going in here?" "Shh," said Fox. "We're home." Jesse's mother was there. Fox said, "We've got one tired buccaneer here." They put him on the bed, and he began crying as they took off his jacket and pants and shoes and socks. "Ow!" Jesse said. His mother wiped his moustache off with a warm washcloth, and she said, "Stop it now. Here, blow your nose." He honked his nose in the washcloth. She tucked him in still in his pirate shirt and underwear.

"How did it go?" she said.

"I don't know if I want to go next year," said Fox.

"Why?"

"I'll tell you later."

"Did Jesse like it?"

"I think so, up until the end. I'll tell you about it."

Jesse started crying again.

"Shush," his mother said. But Jesse could not stop sobbing. "I dreamed I was in Hell," he said.

Fox sat on the edge of the bed and stroked his son's messy hair. "It's okay," he said. "We're home now."

PERJURY

I

The week following his release, Oakes was often gone all evening, and the children were afraid when they went to bed. It was May, almost summer, still light outside at bedtime and long afterward. "What's he doing?" Travis asked his mother, and she said, "Just out unwinding somewhere." Kelly ran her finger along the top of his headboard and examined the dust, fine and sifted, like the ashes of Granddaddy Reynolds after he was cremated and sprinkled from a boat in the Columbia River. "He won't get in any trouble. He don't dare."

Oakes was delaying returning to work. He told his family, "I don't want to just go traipsing in to work a couple days after the trial and be the talk of the mill; all them guys nudging you and joking about it." Everyone was watching him. He said, "Just like my family. Bunch of jokers. Look at everybody smile."

Travis was in fourth grade, and the impression of dislocation was as bad in class as at home. Time remained static and permitted only lateral movements, and those included recess and kids making fun of others and playing kick-ball on the playground and still choosing him first no matter what had happened, because he was so good, and he would return to class with his hair damp and sweat trickling in his ears, having run so hard his lungs tasted fiery, and he sat in his chair by the heater and smelled the chalk and the dusty school ventilation, and saw the wind flutter the young leaves on the trees outside the window, and suddenly the sickening sense returned. He was in the same fragment of time now, at ten-thirty, as he had been when he got up this morning. Mrs. Buckmaster finished taping the map to the chalkboard and said, "See? Like a giant cookie with a bite taken out of it, and in the center is the South Pole."

At home he would close the door of his room and lie on his bed and stare at a poster of a robot with two laser guns and goggles and a titanium breastplate and steel face. Nothing could penetrate his armor. He could ravage the universe with fire. Everything was rushing. Travis got up and unplugged the clock and plugged it back in. Now the digits flashed on the black plastic clockface: oo:oo.

Red-blinking numbers. They did not electrocute my dad.

He remembered Oakes asking what time it was, saying he did not see the red letters so good in the dark.

Travis dismissed the memory and whispered, no longer aware of the habit: "Rap. Rap. Puh puh puh. Ssst ssst ssst." The phrase had become an incantation that had never left his head since the arrest.

Kelly knocked on the door, and when Travis ignored her she entered anyway and sat on the foot of the bed. She said, "What are you thinking?" Travis said, "Nothing." In fact it was nothing. He thought so hard, and there was only nothing, just zeros, double double zeros—*doubloons*, he called them—flashing now on the black clockface in a sound like an explosion in a comic. *DOUBLOON!*

Kelly said, "Look at me, honey. You want to watch some TV?"

"No. Is Dad there?"

Now she was looking at the window. "No, he's gone out somewhere. Come on. We can have some ice cream."

She hugged him, and he held his mother and rested his head on her shoulder. Her face was sallow and unpretty.

Then Kelly said, "Look at your clock. It got unplugged again. How come that keeps happening? I told you not to play underneath that desk."

She released Travis and looked at her watch and set the clock.

"Don't mess that up," she said. "I don't want to keep resetting it."

The rising dread and panic had become familiar since the day his father's mug shot had made the front page of the paper, and he could not shake the image: the empty eyes half closed because of the photographer's flash, the concrete wall behind Oakes, the inmate's number on the card he held, the tips of his fingers pinching the card as if he did not want to dirty them by holding it firmly. Sometimes that face came to him when he was in school. The impression required all his powers to dislodge it, so that even when the teacher looked straight at him, saying his name in exasperation, he was unable to apprehend her question, and she would finally say, "Travis, for heaven's sake, who have we been talking about for the past week? Be quiet, people. Travis? Their names are the same as the bridge across the Columbia to Rainier. Oh, for goodness sake. Anyone else? Lewis and Clark, that's right."

At night, Travis and Darcy would toss about in the covers that were too hot and heavy and hindered sleep as the weather got warmer, but they insisted on keeping their winter blankets, the weight of substance and security upon them, and Travis would cover his head and raise his knees and imagine himself buried deep in a catacomb while missiles rained down on the earth miles above. He was safe.

The front door slammed as Kelly and the children were preparing to pray. They looked at her, and she wiped her palms on her blouse and said, "Shhhh. Just be quiet. He'll go out in a minute." But Oakes came in the room laughing, and he leaned over and kissed them, and his breath was sour and beery. He roughed up Travis's hair. The boy made himself giggle. The windows were bright, and the cracked panes were patched with clear tape that gleamed like strips of gold leaf on an altar, and the Venetian blinds fractured the light horizontally. Kelly stepped back against the wall and nodded when Travis looked at her. Her look seemed to urge him. Travis hugged his father.

"Hey-hey," Oakes said. "Look what I got from this one. Attaboy. Good night, Travesty," and though Travis hated that name, he said only, "Good night." The boy's heart was racing. Oakes sensed his fear and became angry, and that night in a rage he slugged the walls out in the hallway, a thumping that caused implosions of light as Travis closed his eyes and his mother and sister trembled.

Oakes and Kelly had always quarreled, but the shouting matches were better than the way it turned out after the trial, with Kelly silent and afraid to say a word, and Oakes, after an initial few days of watchful remorse, reasserting his dominance, entirely unopposed any longer. Last fall, Travis could hear them up the block as he walked home from school, alone, so he would not have to laugh with the kids at the cartoon sounds of crashing pots and voices yelling streams of ampersands and asterisks. He came in the back door and found them striding back and forth and gesturing theatrically like foreigners, and when the door closed behind him, Oakes said without hesitation, "And the kid's coming with me. Aren't you, Ace?"

"Oh, no, he's not. Goddamn it, Marty, he's staying right here. I'm not having you take—"

"We'll be back in an hour."

"—him out running around God only knows where and having him carouse with—"

"Carouse! Shit. He's ten years old."

"—yes, carouse, with you and your pals and learn your tricks—"

"Jesus! What are you talking about, fucking trained-monkey tricks? Ooka, ooka, ook!"

"—I'm talking. I'm talking. And learn your tricks and your drinking and your smoking dope and whatever else you and your pervert friends do."

"You watch your fucking lip, lady. Pervert."

They were silent, and Oakes seized the moment to say, "So why don't we let him decide? Do you want to go out with the men, or you want to stay home with this old witch?"

"Witch! Don't you call me a witch in front of my children."

■ As Travis and his father pulled out from the curb in the Bronco, Kelly appeared in the living-room window next to the chimney. Oakes did not notice, and the droplets on the panes obscured her, so that her face was only a fleshy smudge framed in mullions and bright maple leaves. Oakes and Travis cruised around town in the rain, and Oakes turned on the wipers only when the windshield got so rain-spattered you could hardly see. The wipers swept the water away, and Oakes turned them back off.

He stopped at a store and told Travis to wait in the car. The boy could see him inside, through the Washington State seal on the window, standing with his hands in his hip pockets as he surveyed the shelves full of bright-labeled bottles as multifarious and pleasing in form as the figures of Magi from a land where colorful robes and turbans are worn. He returned with a bottle in a paper bag, and they drove a few blocks and parked on a levee overlooking the swift, marble-surfaced Cowlitz River, sandstone-colored with the grit that washed off the flanks of the volcano. Oakes said the river had once been clear and green and deep, and power-boats would whine upstream on summer days. "That was when you was just a baby. Before Helen blew. God, was it really that long ago?" They sat with the windshield wipers off and let the car steam up. Oakes tore away the brown paper and unscrewed the cap, and the smell made Travis sneeze. Oakes swigged at the bottle. The drink was the color of tea, and the bottle was dusty. Oakes urged Travis to try a sip.

"Drink up. Come on. You never tasted nothing like that in your entire life. Tastes like fire."

Travis started to raise the bottle to his lips, and Oakes patted him. "A small sip. Start small. That'll scorch you down inside in your little belly."

Travis sipped the whiskey and swallowed fast, and it scalded all the way to his stomach. He coughed, and his eyes and nose ran.

Oakes thumped him on the back. "Good boy. What do you think, Injun Joe? Heap good firewater?"

"Yeah."

"You want another hit?"

"No, sir."

"Strong stuff."

"Yeah."

Oakes massaged his bad shoulder and then gulped from the bottle. "Your mom is trying to turn you against me. Did you know that? You're probably too innocent to realize. You aren't going to let her do that, are you?"

"No, sir."

Travis's stomach was still burning, and his arms began to tingle and warm. For an instant he was inexplicably happy.

"Don't tell Mom about me letting you drink this. You won't tell her, right? Promise?"

"I won't."

"Swear?"

"I swear."

"I'd hate to have to thrash you. I'll do it, too. I'll whup you good. You won't know where to hide."

The car was getting cold. Tears formed on the steamy glass, trickling and leaving clarified, meandering trails like tributaries on a map. The boy put his hands between his thighs to warm them.

Oakes swigged at the bottle. His cheeks bulged and bubbles rose in the bourbon as he drank. Then he said, "Want another taste? Warms you up."

"No, sir."

"Oh, you'd rather just shiver, I guess. This guy likes to be cold. Come on. Here. Small sip, remember. That's right. Hoo-boy, sneezing fit, there. You all right? Don't tell your mother."

Travis said he would not tell. Oakes wiped a porthole of steam in the window and looked across the river.

"Travis, you're my only buddy. Your sister and mother, they don't understand guys like us. But you and me are pals."

Travis's whole body felt warm, and he hugged his father, bumping Oakes so that bourbon spilled in his hair. He was afraid his father would be angry, that he would come home reeking of booze and infuriate his mother, but Oakes kept holding him and saying, "I like that. You hug good, Travesty."

■ The morning after Oakes slugged the wall, the children studied the fist holes in the plaster by daylight, craters in the white plane that stretched for hundreds of miles like an Antarctic desert if you put your cheek to the surface. "What are you doing?" Darcy said.

"Shh!" Travis hissed. "Don't talk by the stairway."

"But why are you—"

Travis clamped his hand over her mouth and whispered, "Shut up! Do you hear me? Do you want to wake Dad? Do you? You know what he'll do if he gets mad."

Darcy became quiet, and she cried silently as she followed him around the kitchen and poured cereal in her bowl and added milk, more in imitation of his task than out of any desire for breakfast. She followed him into the den, where he turned the television on low and flipped through the Sunday morning church broadcasts.

When Oakes came down and sat on the couch behind them, his knuckles were swollen and bruised. He drank beer and tomato juice for breakfast.

"Look at that guy. Shouting and working up a sweat. 'You're all going to hell.' What a dick. Why do you guys watch this stuff, Travesty? Isn't there anything better on?"

Kelly appeared in the doorway eating an apple.

"What a hangover," Oakes said cheerfully. "I think I'm still drunk. That's never happened to me before."

The children, who were sitting on the floor, quietly ate their cereal, spooning out the colored circlets from the lakes of pink milk, for they hesitated to pick up their bowls and drink in the presence of their parents. Travis glanced at his father. Oakes lifted the curtain and stared out the window.

"I think I'm going to work Tuesday," Oakes said. "Start out on graveyard. What do you all think? What does my opinionated family think? God, I'm hungry. I'm so hungry I could gobble up my kids like a big native cannibal man." With his foot he nudged Travis in the small of the back. "What do you think, big chief? What do you say you and me leave the womenfolk and powwow this afternoon?"

2

Sometimes Travis remembered the arrest and thought, What if he had never come into my room at night? Where would he be now? I was asleep. I didn't know what time I woke up. No, I knew and I told the judge the truth. If I didn't say, Dad would be— If I didn't, it would be my fault whatever happened.

All detentions open permanent wounds in families, but arrests that happen at night are the most stark and painful. Travis never would have guessed what was coming when his father woke him up earlier that night. Oakes sat heavily and creaked the mattress, and he leaned over and said, "Hey, Travesty. Wake up, kid. Come on."

Oakes shook Travis and nudged him until he stirred and sat up. It was cold, and the boy held the blankets around his neck. Oakes was calling him "killer" and asking about his bedtime, and at first Travis thought his father was angry because he had gone to bed too late, and he did not understand why his father would wake him to say this.

Travis said, "I went to bed at nine."

"Nine o'clock, you said?"

"Yeah."

"Good boy." Oakes was not angry. He was shivering. "See the clock there?"

"Yeah, Dad."

"What time is it? I can't read those red letters so good in the dark."

Travis rubbed his eyes and said, "Time?"

"Yes, genius."

"Ten o'clock."

"Good boy. Give me a big hug."

The smells of sweat and beer and marijuana smoke clung to Oakes's clothes, but there was also a faint hint of a woman's scent. His shirt was halfway unbuttoned, and there was a cold sweat on his chest and red marks on his skin.

Oakes said, "I just came home, and I'm going up to bed in a little bit. Hey, why don't you get up for a minute?"

Oakes led Travis through the dark living room, walking with his arms extended. He kicked over a three-legged stool and cursed himself. He hobbled to the kitchen, and they sat at the table. Travis slid low in his seat and put his feet on the heating vent to warm them. He dragged his toes across the flutes, and they made a musical noise. Oakes thought a moment, then got a soft drink from the refrigerator and grabbed a tumbler out of the cupboard and filled it for Travis. He set the glass down too quickly, and it tipped and spilled froth across the table. Oakes said, "Aw, hell," and he snatched a towel from the refrigerator handle. He wiped the table and flung the towel in the sink and refilled Travis's glass.

"So what you been doing tonight?"

"Sleeping," Travis said.

"Sleeping. Right, smart ass. I like that. Ask a stupid question—" Oakes was looking around, and he got up and closed the curtains. They sat wordlessly for a minute.

Oakes said, "You haven't drunk nothing."

The taste was disagreeable in Travis's sleep-soured mouth: sugar and carbonation, tickling his nose. Oakes stood and walked around the kitchen and sat down and said, "So you say you went to bed at your regular time?"

"Yeah."

"So you've only been asleep an hour."

"Um, yeah."

"Look at this guy. His eyes are dropping in his head. You want to go back to bed?"

"That's okay."

"So what did you do tonight?"

"Watched TV."

"What did you watch? Something funny?"

"I don't know. Some movie Mom wanted to watch."

"Your mom, eh? Did she say anything about me being out tonight?"

"No, sir."

"You sure?"

"Yeah."

"Surprise, surprise. Well, I wasn't out so late, was I, now? Ten o'clock."

"No, sir." The air felt heavy to Travis, much later than ten, but he did not argue.

"You go to bed. You're getting so tired you can hardly keep your eyes open."

"Okay."

"Here, I'll finish that for you."

Travis returned to bed and listened to Darcy breathe huskily, and after a while he heard shuffling and scraping noises out in the house.

His father paced in the living room, and something clunked against the wooden edge of the couch, and from his bedroom just around the corner Travis smelled bourbon. The hall door was open, and his father whispered, and at first Travis thought his father was speaking to him. Psst, he was saying. Psssst. Travis almost answered, "What?" Then it was quiet for a moment. The springs in the couch creaked. There was a caesura— and they creaked again as Oakes got up and resumed pacing. The faint smell of bourbon came, and Travis's mouth watered. His eyes burned with exhaustion, but he was not sleepy. The soft drink made him thirsty. His father was whispering audibly now: "Shit. Shit. Shit. Shit. Fucking Goddamned son of a bitch."

He stopped suddenly and came down the hall, and Travis closed his eyes. His eyelids were pale and orange. They darkened as his father came to the doorway and blocked the light. "Travis?" he whispered. The boy did not stir. His father entered the room, and Travis's eyelids grew lighter. Something got knocked off the dresser top. Darcy was breathing with rasping noises in the back of her throat. "Travis?" Travis said nothing. "Sweet dreams, killer."

Down the hall in the bathroom, the bathtub tap ran, and a bucket filled with water. Footsteps plodded along the corridor, and the living-room door opened and closed. After a while the footsteps returned, and Travis heard the bucket sloshing into the toilet, and the toilet flushed itself. There were other small noises—the heat turning on, the water running in the bathroom down the hall, his father's careful creeping up the stairway. At the top of the stairs he turned off the hall light, and it was pitch black.

Travis waited until his father had gone to bed before he went to the bathroom. The floor was wet, and in the dim light through the window he descried a bucket in the bathtub. Travis was going to leave the bathroom light off so the brightness would not hurt his eyes, but he had missed the toilet so many times peeing in the dark that the wallpaper was yellowed and peeling, and his mother had yelled at him the last time she found a puddle on the floor; so he clicked on the switch. He lifted the lid and urinated carefully in the toilet and flushed it. He turned out the light. Then his heart raced as his eye retained the image of a white smooth surface like a china saucer, and he turned the light back on. The clock on the windowsill said it was one-fifteen. It was an old electric clock, buzzing like an alarmed stink beetle.

Travis ran to the kitchen, and the clock there now read one-fifteen, though he and his father had sat at the table only a few minutes ago. Maybe I slept and I didn't know it. Maybe we were up longer than I thought. We talked at the table for a long time and I didn't notice.

In his bedroom the digital clock did not give any time. Instead it was flashing 00:00, again and again, and Travis climbed into bed and crawled beneath the covers, taking refuge in the absolute black.

■ The light made the boy's eyes ache.

Darcy's bed was messy and furrowed, and the sheets were exposed and tea-colored in one spot where she had wet the bed, but no one was there. There was a shuffling, and a toy tumbled out of the closet. Kelly was wailing in the hallway.

"Lookit," Kelly cried. "Lookit."

Something cracked, and someone muttered in the closet.

"I can't believe it," Kelly said.

A policeman came out of the closet holding a white object. He did not look at Kelly standing in the doorway. "This is your *Discovery*?"

"What?"

"The toy from the closet in there."

"Yes, sir."

"That's a nice one. Nice space shuttle."

"Thank you."

"My boy has one of those. He's a little younger than you, though."

"Oh."

"I accidentally stepped on it and cracked the tail. I am sorry about that."

Kelly cried from the hall, "He's breaking them. He's breaking your brother's toys."

"A little model glue ought to fix it."

Travis nodded.

The policeman went back into the closet, and Kelly held Darcy in the hallway. Darcy was awake now, and she was crying in her mother's arms.

"Just look at what he's doing. They took your daddy away."

She keened the final note: *Waaaaaaaaaaaaaaaaaaaay,* and Darcy sang with her, but Travis felt a surge of possibility that he knew he should not feel.

There was a sound of hangers clicking on the floor of the closet. The policeman was rummaging. "Oops," he said. "Don't worry, nothing broken. Nothing else."

"Lookit," Kelly said. "Look. I can't believe it. I cannot believe it."

Darcy wailed, "Where is my daddy?"

"Your father wasn't even in there tonight, and look what the man is doing. Tearing the room apart."

Another policeman was in the hall, and he put his hand out as if to pat Kelly on the back, then arrested the gesture. "Mr. Oakes says he was, ma'am. Claims he was with his son at the time of the incident."

"Where's my daddy?" Darcy cried. "I want my daddy."

"What incident? Look at that! It's all a lie. Make him stop throwing the children's toys around, I'll call. I'll call."

Travis looked in the closet. The policeman was squatting and shuffling about in a drum of toys.

"What are you doing?"

The policeman said, "I'm sorry about the *Discovery*. It'll glue back just fine. It broke on a seam, see?"

Kelly's voice came from the hallway.

"I told him at least to stay out of the children's room. Look at him. What do the children got to do with this?"

Another officer told her, "You saw the search warrant, ma'am. I'm sorry."

"Where's my daddy? I want my daddy!"

"They arrested your father. They took him away. These men. Look at them."

Darcy's cry rose to a squeal.

Kelly said, "He did nothing. They're trying to make me think things, make us think, and they took him away to jail."

The policeman closed the drum of toys.

"Why were you looking in there?" Travis said.

"Oh, just snooping around."

"What did my dad do?"

The policeman took off his hat and roughed up his flattop. He was very young, and he had a haircut just like Travis's.

"We took him away for a few days. You'll get him back soon. I'm sorry about the spaceship. Your dad can fix it for you. Fix it when he gets out, I mean. He'll be back someday, I'm sure."

The next morning the bucket was still in the tub, and the clock was flashing 00:00. The policeman had never noticed.

3
—

A week after the arrest they got the Bronco back, and it took hours to clean because the police had covered it inside and out with fingerprint dust—an infuriating nuisance to Kelly because, as she would say later, of course they did not find the so-called victim's fingerprints in the car; she never was in this car. Kelly discovered the mess as she started out to meet the attorney, and she came back in the house and told Travis, "Get the bucket down in the basement."

Travis found the bucket not there but in the tub where Oakes had left it, and he filled it with cleaning liquid and hot water and brought it out to his mother where she stood in the cold beside the Bronco with her arms crossed, holding her sweater closed. She had dust on her elbows and the knees of her nylons from crawling around inside. "Damp!" she said, with such quiet anger that Travis dared not ask what she meant. Kelly had Travis fetch two scraps of old towels from the rag bag, and, while she cleaned inside, he washed off the outside, around the doorways, on the back window, and the dust became sticky like paste. The inside was covered with the powder, and Kelly choked and wiped her nose and said, "Climb inside here and help me if you're done outside. Not you, Darcy. Stop horsing around. If somebody gets wet, I'm taking my hairbrush to you; listen, I don't care whose fault it is."

The boy squatted in the back end, scrubbing it out, and the dust turned white and smeared around. He knelt and then sprang up. The carpet was soaking. "It's wet."

"That's what I was telling you. Darcy! Stay down, honey."

"I want in."

"You can't. It's all messy in here. It's soaking wet. I don't know why the hell they had to douse it with water, too."

Kelly scrubbed the seats furiously.

Travis said, "Maybe they didn't get it wet. Maybe Dad got it wet last night."

"Why on earth would your father do that? No, honey. Darcy. Stay down."

"Maybe he was cleaning it."

"Don't be silly." Kelly wrung out a rag and studied the interior. "Do you know why they did this? Do you know why the policemen did this?"

"No."

"They say your father did something bad. They say he hurt a lady. Do you understand?"

"Yes."

"Do you think they're telling the truth?"

"No."

"Good. Because they're liars."

Travis nodded.

"Daddy wouldn't do that, would he? He wouldn't hurt someone like that. I'm not saying he doesn't get mad sometimes, because he does, and so do you, so do I. But he wouldn't do nothing like that. Never. Because he loves Mama too much, he has Mama and he doesn't need to hurt people."

▬ Travis did not have to go to school that day; Kelly said he would not learn anything, anyway. Instead he stayed home and played with his toys. When he found the afternoon *Daily News* in the living room, it had been stripped of its outer sheets, front page and back, and Travis could not find the comics.

Travis asked, "Where's the comics, Darcy?"

Darcy was twirling in her new pink dress.

"Darcy, have you seen the comics?"

"No."

Kelly said, "Darcy, would you stop! You're making me dizzy. You're going to get sick."

"Mom, what happened to the comics?"

Kelly was surprised. "What?"

"Comics. Don't you know what the hell comics are?"

Kelly did not slap him or tell him, No back talk. She said, "Yes, I'll go get them," distant and obedient, in the tone she now used with his father, and she left the room. She was weak and small, and he hated her for it.

She came back with an individual page torn from the paper. She had ripped it hastily, and the margins of the comics were ragged.

"You tore them."

"I'm sorry."

The boy read the comics he liked and also the ones he always vowed not to read. He wadded them up when he was done and threw the paper at the wood stove in the corner of the room, and it bounced off the cast iron.

"Your father asked for you when he called this morning," Kelly said. "He misses his boy. He wants you to visit him this evening."

"And me?"

"Yes, sweetheart. He misses his little girl, too. He wants me to come with both of you this evening."

But they did not visit their father that evening. Kelly went alone and stayed out until late at night, and Darcy cried because she was hungry.

"Shut up," Travis said. "I'll fix you something if you stop whining."

"I'm hungry."

"I know that. Will you wait a second?"

She followed him around sniveling, and he made her a peanut-butter-and-jelly sandwich. Travis sat her at the table and said, "Stay there a minute. Don't follow me. If you stay there I'll give you a prize."

"Where are you going?"

"To the bedroom. I'll be out in a minute."

The boy went up to his parents' room and found the front page torn from the newspaper. There was a picture of his father standing against a wall with lines marking his height, holding a card with a row of numbers on it. The headline read, "Alleged rapist nabbed at home," and a smaller headline beneath it added, "Woman assaulted at knifepoint."

Travis read the story. Darcy said, "What are you doing?" and he jumped. She was standing behind him at the doorway and watching him with a finger in her mouth. Travis knocked her down.

"I told you not to follow me. I told you not to. If you tell Mom I was here you'll get it."

Darcy was screaming, and Travis ran out the back door. It was dark out, and he unlocked his bike in the garage and hopped on it and rode as hard as he could to the corner and then stopped. A mist was falling in the lamplight, and Travis looked at the black streets, thinking, My father. My father. My father. Travis did not know what he intended to do. He had not even brought his coat. He turned and rode back to the house. He crashed his bike in a heap of boxes in the garage and left it without bothering to lock it up. Inside, lying on the floor of their parents' room, Darcy was squealing, kicking, pounding, chewing on the rug.

"Go away!" she cried. "I want my daddy. I don't want my daddy to die."

"He's not going to die. Why do you say that?"

Darcy pounded her head against the floor, and Travis left the room and went to the kitchen. After a few minutes she followed him, crying quietly. A piece of blue thread hung from a corner of her mouth.

"Finish your sandwich."

"I don't want it. I want my mommy."

"She's my mom, too. Don't say 'my mommy.'"

"I don't want to eat. I want my mommy."

Travis made himself a sandwich, and Darcy peeled apart her own sandwich and began licking the peanut butter and jelly from the insides.

"Daddy's not going to die," Travis said. "Why did you say something like that?"

Darcy licked her fingers.

Travis said, "Until Mom's home I'm boss, and I can tell you what to do. I don't want you to talk about that. You be good or I'm telling."

Darcy took a knife and spread some more jelly on her bread, then began to eat from the jar with her knife, and the boy permitted it, for certain transgressions can be overlooked when a great iniquity has shaken a household.

━ By the weekend they were used to the quiet. They went to church on Sunday, although Kelly said she had not gone since she was a girl, and the teacher made the children sit around a table, put their heads down, and think of secret things about themselves to tell God, things nobody could guess by looking at them. Then she read about Moses, Elijah, and Jesus, and the class made paper Transfigurations with cotton balls for clouds. The boy drew the three disciples spindly and small, like cockroaches, irrelevant to the glory. Across the bottom of the page he wrote the words of God from the cloud: THIS IS MY SON, WHOM I LOVE; WITH HIM I AM WELL PLEASED.

At home that afternoon the boy was allowed to light the fire in the wood stove, and he watched the invisible flame move across the newspaper, turning it black and crumbling it into dried rose petals. They sat on the living-room floor holding hands and prayed that the police would stop lying about Daddy. "Make him be innocent," Kelly prayed. "I will give thee everything and even that thought which is in my heart but he must be innocent. Don't let them hurt him in jail." Travis could not imagine someone getting hurt in jail; there you were safe, and the only thing that could happen to you was maybe getting your head caught if you stuck it between the bars to yell at the guards. You had a cot and magazines. It was boring, but that was your punishment.

That night there was no noise except the television and one dog barking out on the street. The children kept the set on, even when they were not watching, because otherwise they heard the wind in the trees and they were afraid. They spread their toys on the floor and arranged them silently into accusing opposite forces like the terra-cotta armies protecting the tomb of the Chinese Emperor. Kelly served bowls of lime sherbet, and Darcy and Travis stuck out their green tongues at each other.

Sometimes at night long after bedtime, Travis awoke and thought, He's home. Then he kept his eyes closed and pretended to sleep and listened, and the furnace turned off, and gradually Travis remembered: He's in jail until the trial, maybe forever if he's guilty.

One night he dreamed he was riding bikes with his father at the beach, on a long sidewalk where the sand kept blowing through the sea grasses and their hair was thick with salt air; his father held Travis's hand as they rode, and they wobbled and tried to stay close together so their grip would not slip. Travis was aware that someone was behind them, not following but guarding the rear, and he felt safe. When he awoke he was happy. He treasured the dream in his heart, keeping it buried, seldom bringing it even to the level of recollection, unless he was alone where he could examine it at leisure without fear of intrusion.

After the initial shock of the arrest was gone and the dull ache set in, the boy remembered the broken space shuttle, and he found it in the closet behind a basket of clothes he had outgrown. The body was not damaged: there was a scuff where the policeman had stepped with his black heel, but the mark came off if you rubbed hard enough. The tail, however, was partially crushed, and it took careful work to restore it. Travis glued it and set it on a piece of newspaper on the shelf by his bed. And as he worked he whispered the rhythm he could not remove from his head, "Rap. Rap. Puh puh puh. Ssst ssst ssst."

When the toy dried, newspaper stuck to the plastic. The newsprint left a shadow on the white plastic, even after he had picked away the paper—fragments of a classified ad: the words *Corvette* and *speed* and the number 72. Everything in his life felt altered, gargantuan in form, rushing at him and accelerating and darting off to the left or right at the last instant as in a space video game.

The boy whispered, "Rap. Rap."

He tried to scrape the newsprint from the tail with a fork, but he only scratched the words. At least he had not glued the toy with that front page spread under it: then he might have had to scrape off only one letter in the bold headline type instead of three words, only an *a* or a *k* or an *r*, but he would know exactly where the letter had fallen in the alphabet of accusation: A in *nab*, K for *knife*, or R for the harsh, sharp sibilant word that he would still contemplate months later, as he lay in bed after school while his mother and sister watched television and ate ice cream, turning and turning it in his head: Rapist. My father is not a rapist.

Travis mouthed the word all day. He was not a reader, and he pronounced it *rappist*. He subdivided and cut the word: Rap. Puh. Ssst. He said it wrong in his head until they visited his father in jail and Oakes said *rapist* over the phone in the visitors' area, but by then the mispronunciation was embedded in his mind.

Travis brought the shuttle into the living room and scraped at the newspaper letters.

"What are you doing with that good kitchen fork?" Kelly said.

Travis ignored her and whispered to himself as he scratched the toy. Puh. Ssst.

Kelly snatched the fork and demanded, "What did you say?"

"Nothing."

"Did you say something about your mother? Did you call your mother a bitch?"

"Nosireebob."

"If you use that smart-aleck tone with me, I'm going to box your ears."

The boy glowered, and his scorn seemed to wilt her, and she took the fork from him and left the room. "Bitch," he said, loud enough to be daring but not to be heard.

■ When they visited Oakes, he was sitting at a counter in a long line of men who were separated from their visitors by a window, so that they had to talk on the phones. The window was made of acrylic, and there were holes burnt in it. Oakes wore white clothes, and when he turned to leave they saw the word JAIL on the back. The sign behind him said NO SMOK-ING, but he puffed a cigarette and tapped the ashes on the floor.

A voice squawked on the intercom, and although the family could not hear Oakes except on the phone, they could hear the intercom on their side of the glass: "Oakes, put out the cigarette."

Oakes ground out the butt on the counter and flung it over his shoulder. He was talking to Kelly through the receiver.

Kelly nodded and told him, "We'll give him a turn in a minute. I got to talk to you. We got to figure out finances."

Oakes talked.

"Well, I just want one minute," Kelly said. "You can see him right here. He ain't going nowhere."

Oakes spoke angrily, and Kelly replied, "All right, for Christ's sake."

She flung the receiver at Travis and started to walk over to the metal door to press the button for the guard to let her out, then changed her mind and returned.

Oakes said the word the right way, and Travis was surprised at the sound.

"You know what they say I did? They say I'm a rapist."

"I know."

"Your mother thinks you don't know. How'd you find out?"

Travis looked at him.

Oakes said, "I know. You don't want her to hear. Let me guess. You read in the paper?"

"Yeah."

"Hey, first guess. You know what a rapist is?"

"Yeah."

"Well, I'm not. They're lying. You understand? Some very bad mother-fuckers want to keep your old man behind bars for good, because I know things. You understand? It's like in a movie."

Kelly said, "Here, Darcy wants a turn. Give Darcy the phone."

Darcy grabbed at the phone.

"Tell your mother to bug off if she's trying to move you along."

"Dad says bug off."

"Good boy. Now, you remember me visiting you? Don't say it. Nod or shake your head."

Travis shrugged.

Oakes looked panicked. "In your goddamn room the other night."

"Oh." Travis nodded. "Sorry."

"Did you mention it to the cops when they asked?"

"Yeah."

Oakes glanced over his shoulder and said, "You remember the time I was there? Don't say it. I don't trust this phone. Hold up your fingers."

Travis held up ten fingers.

"Good boy. Good boy. That's my boy."

4
‒

Oakes stepped off the elevator from the jail each day of the trial wearing a suit and handcuffed to a deputy, and Kelly would meet him there and walk him to the courtroom. They were an odd threesome: Oakes, his wife in her bright dresses, and a uniformed cop in his Smokey the Bear hat, linked at the wrist, or hand in hand, as they walked down the hallway. Some days, Travis got off school and waited on the bench by the courtroom doors, and Oakes winked as he passed. Kelly and her son could not enter the courtroom; a sign on the double doors read, "Witnesses excluded," and they watched flashes of him as long as the doors kept swinging. Oakes was square-jawed and clean-shaven, and he combed his hair back and oiled it flat on his head. Kelly had bought two dresses for the trial, and she alternated them day by day, red and then blue, identical in style and pattern, a sylvan design with garish monotone galahs and koalas amid the leaves.

Kelly could not quite comprehend what was occurring. She would start into the courtroom, and a deputy would touch her on the shoulder and say, "Sorry, ma'am, you're not allowed. You're a witness." Her son tugged on her elbow to restrain her. She looked around her in confusion, glancing up quickly to meet the eyes of those who were crowding through the door, and she gave Travis a brave smile that faded at once. She took up her post by the doorway, sitting on a stiff wooden bench with a slatted back, and waited; she neither read nor knitted, but simply stared the length of the hallway. Sometimes she brought Darcy, who galloped up and down the hall and talked in a loud voice to clerks and typists and traffic court offenders about her daddy, and her brother had to be the one to quiet her and settle her down on a bench with her coloring book while Kelly tried to hear through the doors what was happening inside.

■ The day Travis testified, before he went into court, he threw up in the men's room sink, and his mother made him gargle in the drinking fountain and gave him a breath mint to suck on. He was afraid of the judge, an ancient, ape-like man barely visible over his desk, who would shift his glasses on his nose, peer at a paper an attendant handed him, then squint at the attorney and ask a question. When the judge explained Travis's duty as a witness, he craned his scrawny neck to look down and spoke carefully and slowly in a sharp, low voice, as if he were talking to a grownup. Behind the old man's ear and running into his diaphanous hair was a swath of scarlet birthmarks, which the boy could see when he leaned forward. Travis tried not to look at the judge's head. When the judge sat back in his chair, Travis could not see him over the bench. He expected the judge at any moment to bend over and say, "Now son, you're going to have to stop this lying and tell us what you know."

Oakes's attorney also was intimidated by the judge. When the judge spoke, he listened with his lips parted, and his head bobbed in agreement. When the attorney questioned Travis, he paced back and forth and wadded a silk handkerchief in his hand, like an infantry captain who had torn down a surrender flag from a soldier's bayonet. He asked questions about Oakes coming in late one night, and the boy, trying hard to think what the right answer would be, said either "No" or "Yes," and then added, "sir."

"Why did he get you up?" the attorney asked.

Travis watched his father, who was sitting ramrod straight at the table behind the attorney, and imagined him strapped in an electric chair with leather bands around his arms and chest; imagined a guard throwing a switch that would jolt his eyes open and clamp his jaw shut and singe his hair so it smoked at the ends. He had seen it on television, and he often thought about it.

"Sometimes he does that," Travis said. "He wanted us to drink and talk."

The attorney made a face, and the crowd stirred and muttered, and the boy knew the answer was wrong. The attorney worked the handkerchief in his hand. He waited for the mumbling to subside. "Drink Coke," Travis said.

"Of course," the man said smoothly. "He wanted to talk, you say?"

"Yes, sir. He just wanted—"

"Do you remember what the time was?"

There were two choices of time—three if you included non-time, the flashing 00:00; and Travis said the correct one, the one he said to the policeman and then in the deposition and repeated ever since with increasing fervor because of the stir it created. It was no longer a decision what to say.

"Ten o'clock."

"What time did you say?"

"Ten o'clock."

The boy knew he had answered right, because the man beamed, and turned and said, "And, of course, the jury is aware what time the complainant claims she was abandoned on Industrial Way."

■ Travis and Kelly were allowed into court when the verdict was read, and they sat directly behind the defendant's table. The guards led Oakes back into the room, and Travis pushed his toes against the rail without looking up. Oakes leaned over and mussed his hair and said, "How." The boy did not respond. Oakes then looked blankly at the empty seats where the jury would sit, and he clicked his tongue. He sat beside his attorney, bunching up his jacket in back.

I do not hope my father is going away. I do not hope he will die. I told them about the time, and nothing is my fault anymore. I do not hope he will go to the electric chair.

The bailiff spoke, and the audience rose and then sat impatiently as the judge pushed through his door, moving his shoulders to settle his robe, and positioned himself in his swivel chair. He nodded, and the bailiff left the room and returned a moment later with the jury. The judge dug at his ears and scanned the twelve severely and spoke to the foreman. And although the boy watched the exchange between the men, intent on every word, nothing registered until the foreman said, "Not guilty, Your

Honor," and a din rose in the room. Oakes jumped up and slapped the arm of his attorney, who gaped at the eleven men and one woman in frank surprise. Kelly leaned over the rail, and Oakes laughed and bussed her. Oakes freed himself from Kelly's embrace and grabbed his son and picked him up over the rail, so that Travis was on the criminal's side with his father's breath in his ear: "Hey, we did it, kid! We did it."

5
—

It was still light out, and Oakes was home early, and he came into the room where the windows were bright like an altar screen in the evening sun. Darcy watched in silence when her father hugged Travis. Oakes started to walk over to Darcy, but he stubbed his toe on a toy gas station and kicked plastic cars all over the room.

"Who left the goddamn thing in the middle of the floor?"

They said nothing.

Oakes said, "Answer me. Travis? Darcy? Well, well. Nobody's fessing up, eh? Then we'll get rid of it."

He went to the window and tried to open the Venetian blinds, but he tangled the cords and they would not budge. He tore the blinds from the wall and flung them rattling to the floor. He slammed open the window and tossed the gas station out. Crouching on the carpet, he gathered up the small cars and flung them out in handfuls. He missed two, a red Corvette in the middle of the carpet and a green truck that he had stepped on and crushed.

Kelly said, "Marty."

"Nobody's toys?" Oakes said. "Then we got rid of them."

He knelt and wrapped his arms around Darcy and growled softly like a cat, and he put her hands on his shoulders, as if to push him away.

"Real somber, huh?" Oakes said. "Somber girl. She won't even give her own daddy a smile. Not even one little smile."

Darcy watched him.

"Come on. Let's see you smile. Or is all you do cry? Are you just a crybaby? I bet you smile for your mama. Come on, crybaby."

Darcy stared at him, eyes wide. She wiped her nose with the back of her hand.

"I'll tickle her. I'll make her laugh. Tickle, tickle, tickle."

Kelly shifted and started to step from the wall but returned with her hands flat against the surface behind her.

Oakes worked Darcy with his rough thick fingers, and she writhed and said nothing, her face contorted. He tickled her and she whimpered.

"What's the matter? Don't you know how to laugh? Can't you laugh here? She thinks her daddy's guilty. She thinks her daddy belongs in jail, don't she?"

Kelly did not stir from the wall. "Marty. Don't."

Oakes kneaded the girl fiercely. Darcy shrieked. Oakes snatched a pillow and padded his fist with it and thumped her in the nose. Her face turned scarlet and ugly, and she cried.

"Marty, stop it!" Kelly grabbed his arm, and he shoved her away and clenched his fist.

Then he let his arm drop and said, "Won't let me play with my own kids. Jesus Christ. It don't matter what a court of law says, your own god-damn family tries and hangs you."

He lifted Darcy up.

"Hey, hey. Come here. Give me a hug. Come on."

Darcy hugged her father and sobbed on his shoulder. He disengaged himself and put her down. Oakes started to leave, but he saw the look on his son's face. "Are you afraid? My old buddy isn't afraid of his dad, is he?"

"No, sir."

Oakes raised his hand as if to swear on oath. "How." Travis smiled. Oakes tickled Travis, and the boy squirmed.

"Nobody's laughing today. Not very funny, I guess."

He walked out, and the wall thumped as he slugged it. In the hall-way he was yelling, "I'm guilty, okay? Is that what everybody in this family wants me to say? God damn you, Kelly, I done it, okay? That make you happy? Fucking ingrate kids, wife." The wall thumped. There was a pause. Then Oakes's footsteps fell away, and a crash came from another part of the house.

The back door slammed, and the car started up outside and screeched off.

As Kelly watched Oakes through the window, she said, "I don't know why you have to set him off like that," and the children cried. She sat beside Darcy and made them bow their heads. "God, make him stop it," Travis prayed. "Make him stop punching Mom and Darcy, and tickling us and everything. Make him go away." Kelly's face stiffened, and she put her fingers on Travis's lips and said, "Shh. Don't say that. He's your father." Darcy kept crying quietly through the prayer time until Kelly said, "That's enough. Now shut up!" and Darcy lapsed into indignant silence.

But Travis insisted, "Why is he like that?"

"Don't ask that. He's your father."

"Why does he have to do stuff to us?"

"It's hard for him after the trial. Everybody thinks— He doesn't have any friends anymore. What he said, he didn't mean it. It's called sarcasm. He's stressed out."

"I still don't see why."

"Why?" said Darcy, repeating it mindlessly as a mantra. "Why, why, why?"

"You two be quiet and go to your room and get ready for bed or I'll paddle you good. Not one peep."

Kelly was already in her nightgown with the sleeves pushed up around her elbows, and through the fabric the boy could see the peaks of her nipples, the indentation of her navel, a dark triangle of pubic hair. When she leaned over to hug Darcy, her nightgown hung open at the neck, revealing her breasts to him. She stared blankly at her son, then noticed his stare and glanced away.

"You worry me," she said. "I don't trust that look in your eye."

■ That night the boy could not sleep, and he tried to recall the dream of the beach and riding bikes with his father, but he could not retrieve the comforting mood. He rose and wandered around the lightless house, weaving through the ghostly forms of stuffed chairs as if guided by an innate recognition: this couch, this footrest, this hallway where I must turn by instinct as I make my way through the swinging door, these fiber-edged fist holes where Dad was punching tonight, this life predicted in advance, foretold action by action, somewhere distant, engraved on the scepter of God. In the kitchen he climbed on the counter next to the sink and knelt in the droplets of cold water that soaked through his pajamas. The tile hurt his knees. He opened the small cupboard that ran along the ceiling above the sink and surveyed the collection of bottles by the moonlight through the window. There were two tones of drink at night: gray and clear. The brandy would taste sweet, but there was only a thin syrup dried on the bottom of the bottle. His mother had noticed the last time he drank the Irish Cream and had blamed his father, though not to his face. Travis picked up the bottle, the body, the torso, and longed for the smooth cool sticky liqueur. He nearly dropped it in the sink and kept himself from gasping in the rush of horror that followed. He shoved the bottle back in the cupboard. Then he found, hidden in the dark at the back of the shelf against the wall, the bourbon, which Oakes drank in such quantities he never noticed anything was missing. The boy hopped down and opened another cupboard and got out a cup, the one, he could tell by the shape, that bore the legend, "Thou shalt not bullshit." He poured himself a shot and turned on the tap and ran the water over his wrist until it was icy, then added some to the drink.

Whispering, "Rap," stuck on the syllable, unable to move on: "Rap."

THE SKY RANCH

THE MORNING WAS HOT, AND THE DRIZZLE, WHICH HAD SPATTERED
the windshield as Judith Kettler drove, grew faint and then ceased alto-
gether by the time she reached the Zenith Sky Ranch. The trees shifted
almost imperceptibly beyond the airstrip, but high above, a strong wind
pulled apart the cloud ceiling and shuffled swatches of humid blue. Judith
waited at the door to the hangar. It occurred to her that she was holding her breath. Everyone was looking for Ray Sikorski, the skydiving instructor.

"He'll be your tandem," someone said. "He's great. He's just a little
late sometimes."

The wait annoyed her. She had gotten up at six, left her husband,
Charlie, asleep in bed, and driven from Chicago to this airstrip near
Genoa, and suddenly she wanted it to be over and to be on her way home.
Judith was a former maternity ward caseworker assigned to visit homes
after babies were born, but she had been jobless since the move from her
Columbia River hometown earlier this summer. She was tall—over six
feet—and had a ruddy Scottish face that blushed easily, in blotches, and
ears that glowed red when she was nervous, as now. Lately she had given
up the look she had carried, with small accommodations to changes in
style, since she had gotten her first job out of college a decade ago, in
1978—stylish skirts or suits, colorful blouses, shoulder-length hair—and
in her unemployment she affected a less formal and possibly more forbid-
ding look: jeans, frumpy blouses, black leather boots. She had also had her
hair cut short and stopped dyeing it to hide the early threads of gray. On

the small of her back was a kanji character that a tattooist in Lincoln Park had insisted meant "chaos" but which a Japanese at the YMCA's women's self-defense class had translated as "gathered in a group," to Judith's embarrassment. The character had caught her eye because she and Charlie had honeymooned in Japan, and it angered her to get it wrong in such a permanent way.

Judith sat at a picnic table just inside the hangar, where the women had laid out submarine sandwiches and a box of fried chicken and a portable salmonella factory in the form of a bucket of sweet macaroni-and-onion glop that someone had bought at a gas station deli in Genoa. The rafters were decorated with streamers of red, yellow, blue, white, and green, as if someone had run an elementary school's flags-of-the-world project through a lawn mower. Several people were checking the lines of the multicolored parachutes stretched out on the concrete floor. They sometimes glanced at Judith; apparently the Zenith Sky Ranch was a clannish organization that did not often draw strangers.

When she had tried out the idea of skydiving on several new acquaintances in Chicago (it could not yet be said that she had friends after only six weeks in Illinois), everyone said, "Whoa!" and "You go, girl," and had stories of past adventures to tell, about bungee jumping or paragliding or being towed behind a boat in Acapulco while hanging from a parachute. Charlie, however, had set down the front section of his Sunday *Trib* when she mentioned it to him last weekend and regarded her with alarm.

"Why skydiving all of a sudden?" he asked. He did not say, as he once might have, teasingly, "Are you mad, woman?" He was a careful and considerate man, and he had taken to weighing his words in her presence as one tests a rickety chair before settling into it, a sign, if she needed one, that she was still fragile. "Judith, I'm sorry, but I don't have any interest in jumping out of a plane."

"You don't have to go if you don't want."

"Well, of course I have to."

"Why?"

"I can't just let you—. No. Start over. I don't mean 'let you.' What I'm trying to say is, I'd want to support you in whatever you decide to do, within reason, I mean, short of—. But, honey, this is dangerous. Besides, you can't just drive out to O'Hare some afternoon and jump out of a plane. It takes months of lessons and leaping off platforms and learning to roll and all that. So I've read."

"You're wrong about the lessons. This is tandem jumping. No lessons are required because you're harnessed to an instructor and he or she pulls the ripcord. And yes, I think I'll pass on jumping out of jet airplanes at America's busiest airport, since there's this Zenith Sky Ranch, they call it, over near Genoa. Somehow I liked the name."

Charlie asked her for more details, studied the ad she had found in the aviation newsletter left on the treadmill at the YMCA, and said nothing more about it until later that afternoon when they took Cecil, their Rhodesian Ridgeback, for a walk in their Andersonville neighborhood. They were admiring the leafy streets and the mix of brownstones and brick condos, still strange and attractive to their eyes, accustomed, as they were, to wood-frame houses over-loomed by tumors of pulp-mill steam, and to orienting themselves by the green, serrated ridges beyond the rooftops rather than by the black tombstone of the John Hancock Center. A drumbeat sounded somewhere nearby. She assumed it was a panhandler pounding on a plastic tub and hollering, "Spare change?" But then they rounded a corner, and the noise resolved itself into something wooden and ancient, Japanese drumming, coming from behind the Buddhist Temple of Chicago. Prayer flags fluttered on the walls, and the beat was deep and heartrending. Judith recalled their visit to Sado Island during their honeymoon, the oyster-eating contest, the bright sea, the middle-aged women dancing in their blue kimonos, the men in headbands banging on enormous drums hanging from frames as ornate as Korean temples on wheels.

Charlie steered her into an alley where she would not be seen by two families heading toward the temple. "Give me the dog. The dog! Are you all right? Why don't we go home?"

She blew her nose. "No, I'm fine. Just remembered Sado."

The dog tensed as a squirrel scurried up a tree, and Charlie said, "Cecil!" and tightened the leash around his fist. "I won't ask you to give it some thought, because I'm sure you have and you will. This skydiving plan of yours. But you should be careful, that's all, and it's obvious you don't need the stress."

"It isn't stressful. It's just something to do. I'm bored."

"I think you don't need this right now."

At once the squabble over something as ridiculous as skydiving made her tired. "Maybe you're right."

But all week the thought of falling—simply falling in silence—gnawed at her, and this morning, a Saturday, she willed herself to wake at five-thirty a.m. without an alarm, and got up to drive to the Zenith Sky Ranch.

Before departing she wrote a note on a sheet of perforated paper torn from the printer and left it on the kitchen table for Charlie: "Out for the morning. Back by 1. Love you." But then a terror seized her—a certainty that she was going to fall to her death—and on a second sheet she scrawled a farewell letter, just in case, to be read posthumously. She told Charlie she loved him and thanked him for being so wonderful and supportive, especially during the nightmare of this past year; it was hard on him, too, she knew, especially the way the trial had ended, but he had been a rock for her, and he should know that she was not unhappy with him but simply had reached a point where she needed to do this. She slipped it in an envelope on which she scrawled, "To be opened only in the event of my death." For a moment she considered where to leave it: somewhere Charlie wouldn't find it this morning but also would not fail to discover it by the end of the day should she leave a Judith-shaped hole in a cornfield somewhere. She settled on the mailbox: he would not check the mail until late afternoon, when the postman came; and assuming she survived she would be home long before then.

Now, as she sat at the picnic table in the hangar, a yellow plane buzzed overhead like a wasp and excreted a number of specks. Judith followed the others outside to watch. Rectangular parachutes opened across the sky and drifted earthward with surprising speed, but one chute did not fully open and the skydiver corkscrewed in the air as he fell. Everyone gasped as the parachute broke free and drifted away like a handkerchief flung into the wind, and the diver sped up in his fall. His reserve parachute opened, an old-fashioned hemisphere, red- and white-striped like a beach umbrella or a circus tent. He disappeared in the trees beyond the field.

Several men jumped into two pickups and raced to the field where the divers landed. The first truck returned within minutes; it was followed sometime later by the other vehicle, where a skydiver was sitting in the bed, his face scraped and bruised and with an armload of nylon in his lap.

He was barefoot and his feet were red and swollen. His shoes lay beside him.

The driver told the people who gathered, "Had to cut him out of the trees. Tore his reserve all to hell."

"The reserve don't matter," said the skydiver. "It's the regular chute I'm worried about. Five thousand dollars. It drifted across the highway."

Someone tugged at Judith's elbow—a fat, bearded pilot who introduced himself as Spook; she was not clear if this was merely a nickname or something he would sign in the presence of a notary. He wore cutoffs that left his plump, hairy legs exposed, and high-top tennis shoes on which he had drawn skulls-and-crossbones with a permanent marker.

"I found Sikorski," he said as he led her around the hangar. "Sorry for the delay. He was in the trailer. I checked earlier but I didn't notice him on the floor behind the bar. He had a bad day yesterday and I guess he was just sleeping it off. His son was supposed to jump with him, but he chickened out."

"Oh?" Judith sang in a modulating voice that revealed her nervousness.

"Not like I'm trying to scare you off. See—"

But by now they had arrived at the trailer, and Spook said, "Anyway, Sike's a great guy. I'll see you out at the plane."

Inside she met Sikorski, a silver-haired truck driver and former paratrooper whose face was scarred with a bad case of rosacea. He sat at the bar drinking a beer. He reminded her of her father, a paper mill supervisor, until he spoke in some kind of Chicago mobster accent that pronounced *this* and *them* "dis" and "dem." He had a black eye and swollen lip, and the carpet had imprinted a fossil pattern on his cheek.

"Sorry for the delay." In an attempt to make himself presentable, Sikorski roughed up his hair. "Took a little catnap this morning. Late night."

Sikorski gestured for Judith to sit in an easy chair across the room, then plugged a cassette into a video player. On the screen, a man with the chest-length beard of a bum or a holy fool explained that tandem jumping was experimental and that a mishap could result in serious injury or even death.

"The novice may back out at any point and still receive a full refund," the man said. "No one is forcing you to jump. As soon as you set foot on the plane you consent to this stipulation."

As the video ended, Sikorski stared at Judith's feet, and she shifted uncomfortably before realizing he was in fact eyeing the contents of the handbag sagging open on the floor. She zipped it shut.

"You know how to use it?" Sikorski said.

"Wouldn't do me much good if I didn't."

"Bully for you. But you know you can't take it in the plane."

"Of course not."

"Not trying to insult your intelligence. We just get all types here, is all. So: I've got the legal hocus-pocus for you to sign, and we're good to go. Oh, and it'll be ninety dollars in cash."

The document Sikorski gave her promised that neither the signatory, his/her relatives or friends, or any other person he/she knew or did not know now or in the future would ever sue the Zenith Sky Ranch (hereafter known as "the Provider") should the signatory in any way suffer injury, emotional trauma, or loss of life, whether or not the Provider should be determined to be at fault through equipment malfunction, negligence, or both. It was ridiculously overbroad, and with some amusement she signed on behalf of the entire population of the earth, past, present, and future.

She handed him the paper. "You left out extraterrestrials. They could still sue on my behalf if I die."

Sikorski searched the document for the loophole. "Goddamn lawyers," he said.

From an overhead cupboard he pulled out a set of blue mechanic's coveralls and tossed them to Judith.

"If you need to, you can powder your nose at the ladies' Porta-Potty out back, then slip these on. We'll reconvene at the hangar in ten."

Judith locked the trailer door behind him and donned the coveralls, clean but stained with black grease like a Rorschach test, then headed out to leave her purse in the trunk of her Celica. Inside the hangar, Sikorski handed her goggles and a rubber helmet that resembled a stout shower cap, then showed her how to strap on the harness. Moving behind her, he hitched the straps so tight they hurt her thighs and seemed to compress her spine.

"I tell the guys to get their nuts out of the way, otherwise it can get mighty painful as you hang there. But you don't have to worry about that."

She turned in an attempt to read his expression, but he said, "Hold still," and adjusted a strap on her back.

He led her out to the airstrip, where Spook was gassing up a yellow Cessna Skylane 182 A at a 1950s-era pump, and they stood under the wing as Sikorski reiterated several points he called "absolutely essential, so listen careful now," but Judith was too nervous to attend and simply said, "Yes. Yes, okay," whenever a response seemed to be called for. The fuel pump clattered away but the price never registered; the zeros dithered, as if anxious to surrender their places to ones and then twos and then threes, but alone among all things living and dead they remained trapped in time, clicking, clicking, clicking, never changing, while a swath of sunlight crossed the runway at leisure and shimmered across the cornfield beyond.

Sikorski closed in, chest to her back, and hooked his harness to hers. "This is how we'll be," he said, his hands on her waist. His breath smelled of mouthwash gargled to cover malt liquor, and she gagged, remembering the way Oakes had been sucking on breath mints after drinking, to render himself presentable as he pressed a knife to her throat. Now, a year later, she felt the sinking in her gut, as if she were free-falling many miles toward concrete.

Judith removed Sikorski's hands from her sides. "Don't."

She would not have skydived had she known it would be like this, compressed into one dense space with a stranger; somehow she had envisioned hanging from a tether, yards below him. But now it seemed too late to back out. She wanted to fall.

"We don't have to go through with this," Sikorski said in her ear as he unhooked the harness. "You can back out at any moment until we jump. Full refund."

"It's all right."

She held her breath as he explained one last time that she would climb out first, like so. Then, when he rapped her on her helmet, she'd let go and tuck her arms and legs into almost a fetal position as they dropped away from the plane. When he rapped a second time, she would spread her arms and legs like an X. This was the one thing to remember, even if she forgot everything else.

"If we buffet, it's because you're not doing the X. Arch your back and spread your arms and legs. If we run into trouble, I'll stop the free-fall by pulling the ripcord. I'll remind you how to land once we're in the air."

■ The airstrip ran slightly downhill, toward a grove of shingle oaks and a pasture beyond where cattle grazed, traumatized and milkless, she imagined, because of the buzz of planes passing a few yards overhead every weekend. Spook gunned the engine, and for a horrifying second Judith feared they would not clear the trees, but they wobbled up over the grasping branches with their trembling green and gold leaves, and ascended above the Illinois landscape, so flat to a Westerner's eye, yet pastoral, peaceful. Through bug smears the horizon rose and fell—mostly fell.

Spook occupied the only seat in the cockpit, and Judith sat on a wooden box set on the floor beside him. Sikorski sat on the same box behind her, with his back against hers, and through her coveralls she felt the bulk of the parachute. She slid forward a little. An aerial photographer was lounging in back holding, in his lap, a helmet with a camera attached to the top. Whenever Spook pulled back on the controls, a parallel set thrust out at Judith. Her scalp was growing hot in this idiotic rubber helmet, and a trickle of sweat stung her eyes.

Sikorski stumbled to the back of the plane to speak to the photographer, and Spook glanced over his shoulder before shouting at Judith over the drone of the engine.

"Anyway, I didn't finish telling you about yesterday. About Sikorski?"

Judith glanced back at the skydiving instructor, who was thumping the photographer on the shoulder. Obviously they couldn't hear.

"His kid, Brad, is an ex-con, and not exactly the brightest bulb on the Christmas tree. Tried to rob a strip club in Gary after making use of its, shall we say, lap-dancing services, and he ended up getting shot in the leg and doing time for both robbery and solicitation. Ha, ha! Anyway, he'd never skydived before. Suddenly, he decides to turn over a new leaf, mend fences with Pop. He was even talking about getting qualified as an instructor. But when he got up in the Cessna at ten thousand feet, he froze up. Happens sometimes. Sikorski was not a happy camper. He goes ape-shit, tries to throw him out of the plane."

"Jesus. Was he trying to kill him?"

"No, not like that; I mean, while they were harnessed together. Which, don't worry, he wouldn't do anything like that to you. If you have last-minute thoughts and decide not to, no shame at all. Full refund, no questions asked. But because this was his son, Sikorski took it personal. They're, like, hooked together, and Sikorski's struggling to get to the door while Brad hangs on for dear life and screams, 'Dad, what are you freakin' doing?' Only he didn't say 'freak.' Big tough guy who's done time in prison. I'm like, 'Cool it, you yahoos, we're going to crash.' That settled them down, and Sikorski unhooked their harness. But when we landed, Sikorski up and slaps Brad's face. Smack! So of course Brad hit him back, twice, three times, beats the shit out of his own father, right there on the landing strip, which is why you probably noticed the eye. Sikorski won't press charges, though. His son." Spook mused for a moment, then said, "Skydivers are crazy. Go figure. I wouldn't jump. You'd never get a pilot out of a plane."

Sikorski returned and sat with his back against Judith, and Spook fell silent.

Sikorski said something inaudible, and she smiled. He nudged her and said, "You don't, do you?"

"Good girls don't," called Spook.

She looked out the window. Sikorski tapped her shoulder.

"Ignore him, he's an imbecile."

"So I gather."

"Did you hear my question?"

"I'm sorry, the noise."

"You don't have that Makarov on you now, do you?"

"No, it's in my purse. In the trunk of the car. The only reason I carry it is a friend of mine was raped last fall. Shook me up. When I heard about it, I mean. So I got a gun."

"Don't get me wrong; it's always a pleasure to meet a red-blooded, fully armed American woman, but I don't want it going off when we jump. Bullet through both our hearts. Interesting choice of a firearm, by the way. Russian make."

"I got it cheap."

"The V.C. carried them. The officers, commissars. Their side-arm."

The plane droned higher over the rumpled quilt of pastureland and alfalfa fields and ponds, squared off by roads and marked with the mushroom growths of small-town water towers. Sunlight filtered through the voluminous miasma of a grass fire in the distance. She could see the line of the highway through Genoa and a woodland beyond. A pond glimmered on a farm beneath them. At nine thousand nine-hundred feet they brushed the underside of the clouds and passed through a wisp of fog.

"Can you drop her a hundred feet, couple of hundred?" Sikorski asked, and Spook nodded.

Sikorski lurched over and opened the door of the plane, and the air that rushed in was surprisingly cold. Then, duck-walking around, he helped Judith scoot on the box to face the door. He straddled the box behind her, like an ape preparing to mount her, and clipped their harnesses together. Then he tugged the box out from under them. They wriggled closer to the open door. She was practically in his lap, smelling his liverish breath in her ear.

"Last chance to change your mind."

"I'm fine."

"Good girl. Wait a minute. Hold on. Okay—now. Go on. Step out on the wheel. Go, go, go!"

But somehow she could not move.

"Never mind," said Sikorski. "We'll try again after that other plane's out of the way. You sure you want to do this?"

"I think so."

"No shame in backing out. My pay's the same either way."

"I'm not backing out."

The plane circled around, providing a view, across the fields of Genoa, of brick houses and wooded streets and railroad tracks, and far away across the prairie, she saw the towers of Chicago and the white expanse where Lake Michigan merged with the sky. One's eye kept trying to turn white forms on the horizon into mountains—Rainier, St. Helens, Hood—but they were not glacier and rock but mere particles of airy water that would dissolve into new cloud forms in an hour.

"All right," Spook called. "We're back around."

Judith stretched her legs out the door and stepped out onto the wheel into the wind, and Sikorski followed her. The plane bobbed. He was panting and sweating. She was afraid she would knock her teeth out on the arm supporting the wing if she let go. Then suddenly they were falling into a hurricane.

Tucking into a fetal position, Judith saw the plane recede at an astonishing velocity as the photographer dove out after them. Sikorski thumped her helmet, and she remembered to arch her back and spread her arms and legs in an X.

The winds tugged at her helmet and yanked a leather glove from her hand; and, although she wanted to watch it fall alongside her, it was gone. The pastures below, separated by what resembled miniature hedgerows, were broken continents of light and shadow, and bright with summer mustard. They were buffeting, and she thought, This is it. I'm going to die.

Then a hand covered her forehead. She had almost forgotten Sikorski was here. A hand on the forehead—was she supposed to do something? The chute opened and their fall jerked to a halt. In her harness she hung below Sikorski. Suddenly the air was warm and still. She whooped.

"Grab the reins," he said.

She hooked her hands through a set of loops. The harness pinched her groin and armpits. Far below, another skydiver swooped in his parachute. It was the photographer.

"How did he get down there?"

Sikorski did not hear her. "Look up," he called.

The rectangular chute, red and blue, billowed with air, resplendent in the white void. Again she whooped.

Her arms, however, began falling asleep as she held them overhead.

"Aren't we falling a little fast?"

"No, this is normal."

"Where are we landing?"

"We're shooting for that field, just past the arrow. That shows the direction of the ground wind."

Then Judith saw it: a fifteen-foot-long wooden arrow, painted white. He talked her through the landing—"If you need to, tuck and roll to your side"—then, "Fine," and there was nothing more to say to each other.

For a time they were silent. The air smelled smoky, but she could no longer see the grass fire. Her eyes stung as if somebody had been slicing onions.

A question came from above and behind her: "So I gather Spook told you about my kid?"

It was awkward responding when she could not see his face. "Brad sounds like quite a guy."

"He's an asshole, a complete asshole. Just like his old man."

"Oh, that's not true."

"Why else would he do that in front of all my friends?"

They drifted over a dirt road and an alfalfa field covered with hay bales like squarish vitamin tablets laid out on the faded felt of a pool table. The fields were no longer lined in hedges, but trees; nor was Lake Michigan visible. The branches and the leaves trembled in the sunbeams slanting through the sky.

"Got any kids?" Sikorski asked.

"Someday. Not now. I don't know."

"Someday you'll know. Because, when Brad was a baby, he couldn't sleep unless I sang to him and rocked him for a while in the dark."

He sang with an Irish lilt that sounded strange on his Chicago Slavic tongue:

> "I played a wild rover for many a year,
> And spent all my money on whiskey and beer.

"Stupid songs like that. They work, though; you'll see. It was the best feeling I ever had when he finally gave a little sigh and fell asleep. And so as a dad, you think they'll remember. Not really remember. Know it in their bones. What you did for them. Diapers. Tickling him when he hid behind the curtains. Taking him to see the Sox before he could walk. Then again, I probably was an asshole, made him play Pop Warner football when he kept coming home in tears. 'It hurts.' 'Well, hit 'em back, dummy. You got to be tough.' You, Judy: you're tough, that I can tell. Your gun, I mean. You'd've made a great football player, if you were a man. To play football you've got to know how to absorb and deliver pain."

For a moment they said nothing.

"This friend of mine," Judith said, "she got out of a Library Board meeting, and this guy pulled her into his van and raped her in the parking lot. Then later she messed up the first time she viewed the lineup, picked the wrong guy. Stupid. When she saw the guy in court, she knew it was him. But he had an alibi, it turned out. Of course, the alibi was his own kid, but all this was enough to create doubt."

"So he got off."

She nodded. "So I figured, next time I'll kill the guy. I mean, if that ever happened to me. I'd shoot him, and if I couldn't manage that, myself."

"You know, Judy, I like your style. Okay, pull on your right strap. So: was she married, this lady you know? Boyfriend?"

"What does that have to do with anything?"

"So why didn't her guy kill the son of a bitch?"

She shook her head and felt the back of her helmet thump his abdomen. "You're an idiot. You don't know the first thing, don't understand what it does to both of you. Anyway, you wouldn't kill anyone."

Laughter tumbled down. "Pull, pull, pull. The right one. Yes, I have. Have killed someone. Many someones. I was in Khe Sanh. And I would, they touched my wife. I'm not saying this is right, it's just me. I got a temper. Now, listen up for a minute."

Sikorski directed her through several swooping turns. "Pull left. Good. Ease up—easy, easy, easy. Good."

They crossed the trees—too low?—but by the time she had entertained the thought they were clear. A space opened between the bales, and the field came up to meet them. They landed lightly, on their feet, but then Judith fell over and brought Sikorski down beside her.

He disconnected the harness, then stood and wound the cords around his arm, elbow to palm, while she squatted and plucked foxtails from her socks. The parachute swelled like a jellyfish and tried to billow away. She ran over and held it down for him.

When Sikorski had wound up the cords, she gathered the chute and stuffed it into his arms. She hopped and gave a gleeful kick, almost a dance step.

"Great landing," he said.

Judith began laughing. Clutching her abdomen, she sat on a hay bale and laughed till she was breathless.

"You all right?" Sikorski asked.

"It's nothing. Nice of you to say so. About the landing."

The pickup that had brought back the injured skydiver approached on the dirt road, whipping up a tail of cork-colored dust. Then she saw the dark Volvo following it. Charlie's. Both vehicles stopped, and he came running across the field and hurtled a hay bale. Then she was in his arms.

"My God," he said. "I saw you come down. Are you crazy?"

"Yes, absolutely nuts." Then Judith saw how angry he was, and her gaze fell.

Sikorski approached with the chute bunched in his arms.

"Who's this, the little man? Glad you caught the show. Ray Sikorski. Pleased to meet you. She done good. Better than my son yesterday, that's for sure. She's a natural."

"Good for her."

"Listen, Annie Oakley, you keep up that target shooting. Don't do you no good if you flinch when you fire, which, not to be sexist, but most women do. Novices, anyway."

As the Kettlers walked to Charlie's car, Sikorski got into the back of the pickup with a wad of blue and red in his arms. The pickup turned right, but Charlie headed left, eastward, toward Chicago.

"We've got to return my coveralls and harness," she said.

"Mail them back."

"My car. And my purse is in the trunk."

Charlie braked and swerved onto the shoulder, rattling gravel against the undercarriage.

"Stupid me," he said. "I saw it. I stood there with my hand on the hood while some guy on crutches told me I was too late, you were already up in the air, and by the way, he'd just broken both of his feet. After I found that note of yours. You scared the shit out of me. I thought you meant to kill yourself."

"Oh, Charlie, I'm so sorry. I didn't think you'd find it before I got back. And if I didn't make it, I wanted to say good-bye."

"I just find it incredibly selfish that you would do such a thing without telling me. Did you think I'd handcuff you to the bed if you were intent on going? I told you the choice is yours."

"I thought you'd talk me out of it."

Charlie pressed his forehead against the steering wheel as if studying the sun-cracked vinyl of the dashboard and the slow clicking progression of the second hand on the clock. A wasp was buzzing about inside the car, bumping against the windshield and circling over Charlie's thinning pate, and Judith rolled down her window and brushed it out. It managed to return twice before she got rid of it.

"Charlie," she asked, "have you ever wanted to kill someone?"

They never uttered Oakes' name, but his eyes blazed as if she had reopened an old argument.

"That, and do other things," he said. "Every day. In a way, I think I've become a disturbed man, a shrink would probably say; I'm always having these fantasies of mutilating him. If I cut off his nose and ears, the way the tsars used to punish their enemies, would it be a sufficient retribution for what he inflicted upon you? If he were shunned, stared at, despised for his disfiguration even when he drops that fucking kid off at school or goes to 7-Eleven for a pack of cigarettes. But yes, you're right, killing would be the most efficient, the most just, somehow, the least soiling of the one who dispenses the punishment. You know, I actually saw him in downtown Longview one day a few weeks after the trial, and I followed him. He bought some sort of engine fan in that junk shop on Commerce and then drove down to a tavern on Industrial Way. I followed his goddamned van, the one where—. And—"

Charlie foundered. Now the wasp was trying to reenter the car from outside the windshield, head-butting the glass.

"And, see. The point is—. Focus. I went in and sat down at the bar a few seats down from him and ordered a beer. He had a pitcher in front of him. He didn't recognize me; his back had been to me the whole trial. Tried to talk about the Mariners. I just glowered at him, and although I've never been in a fight in my life, never drawn my fist against anyone, he looked afraid and turned away. The bartender, this woman with a low-cut neckline that he kept drooling over, she was slicing turkey breast for a sandwich, and when she went back into the kitchen for something, she left her knife within reach. I wanted to plunge it into his throat. Every day in my mind I do it. Other things, too. Like, waiting outside his house after work and shooting him in the eye. I actually planned the whole thing out. Drove by his house. It's green, flaking paint. No porch light. He owns it, name is on the title. I watched that lying little shit, his son, sitting on the porch, throwing a pocketknife at the lawn, retrieving it, throwing it again, while sipping from a cup with a couple fingers of apple juice or something. His dad is on at C-shift at the mill, by the way, which means today he's on graveyard. Gets off at six-thirty a.m. Broad daylight at this time of the year. Dogs barking. Mill workers coming home off graveyard."

For a time she absorbed this. "So why didn't you do it?"

"Because I'm not so stupid as to think you could pull off the perfect crime. I mean, come on, I'd be the first person the cops would interview as a suspect. I'm not an actor. They'd see the guilt in my face. The jury would sympathize with me, sure, but they'd send me down for life. Why shouldn't they? Murder one. Or even if it was eight or ten years, you ask yourself, 'What's the point?' Separated from you. That I couldn't take. Losing you."

"You never told me any of this."

"What's to tell? Your husband has rage issues. You knew that."

Judith touched his face, traced the whorl of his ear, which always was sprouting dark hair no matter how often he trimmed it. Somehow she found this quite sexy. Kissing his cheek, she tasted salt on his skin. He reached for her leg but then hesitated, gripped the gearshift. She stroked his knuckles.

The light shone on the fields, on the wisps of camel hair grass and shimmering corn. Far ahead, smoke billowed from a burning field, and she had the strange sensation, as if from a former life, of falling through the scumbled light toward the crosshatch farmland of someplace she did not know.

"It still could be done," Charlie said. "Killing him."

"No. You're right. I need you. He will suffer for what he did. I believe that. Karma."

"What the hell is burning out there? There can't be forests around here, this flat goddamned country. Isn't there a rural fire department?"

Somehow in this mindset the topography itself seemed to be an outrage against him.

"Fields," she said, reassuringly. "They burn off the stubble, I think. You can see it better up there. From the sky. Maybe we should try it together sometime."

For the first time in many weeks, he laughed, and shook his head, as if to say, teasingly, *You're hopeless, you know that?*

Charlie U-turned back onto the road and headed back toward the airstrip. Judith clutched his hand as he shifted gears. No plane was visible, but suddenly a line of parachutes opened up where nothing had been, and drifted in the haze like seed pods released in a fire.

THE WORLD IN THE FIRST YEAR
OF THE WIRE

THE NEW YEAR WAS STARTING OFF SO QUICKLY, WITH SO MANY victories and defeats and newsworthy incidents, we were afraid things were occurring elsewhere and here much more rapidly than ever before. There was so much more to know, and the pages ran together in one's head, and it was hard to tell at first glance which events were occurring somewhere distant such as Chihuahua City, where a Villista army of 5,000 men were within striking distance, and which were in Grants Pass or Merlin or Ferrydale, where Young Cupid was busy last year and pierced the hearts of the beautiful Miss Elizabeth Salvo and the gallant N.R. "Dick" Filips, the warehouse clerk and former star fullback on the Grants Pass High School Cavemen gridiron team that had come so close to qualifying for the state championships before he was thrown from a mule and broke his collarbone, disappointing fans, one and all.

It had never been like this before. "No Other Town in the World the Size of Grants Pass Has a Paper With Full Leased Wire Telegraph Service," the masthead of *The Rogue River Courier* proclaimed, and that explained why we were perhaps unprepared for the furious gales of events. The motto was written by publisher A.E. "Boss" Voorhies himself, and whenever Mr. Voorhies wrote something, you were prudent to read it twice. He was a tall, mole-freckled man who wore a homburg as he strode down the Sixth Street boardwalk each morning on his way to work, touching the brim of his hat with two fingers if you greeted him.

Watching him pass, you found it hard to believe he could be at the fore-front of this revolution in information technology. Swifter and swifter we were drawn into a vortex of news everywhere on the planet, and things far away became mixed with our own families and train schedules and the prices of hogs on the Portland market, and sometimes we did not know if it was here or somewhere distant that bandits waylaid a camel caravan crossing the desert in a scene that surely must have had the lady readers' hearts stopping, Berbers sweeping out of the hills with scimitars and carrying off all the maiden Frenchwomen.

★   ★   ★

WE WERE OUTRAGED. No woman in Josephine County would be safe with Berbers running wild. Men in stained bedsheets and hoods marched through town waving torches, and they got the City Council to post a billboard by the gravel pit that said, "Nigger Beware: Sundown Law." Hooded men set up booths in the snow outside churches to collect signatures for the recall of Sheriff Bill Lewis, who had let crime run amok among Berbers and other Native Peoples. Their voices were dank and familiar beneath the sheets as they called to a burly young man with a scar on one eyebrow who was escorting his lovely if visibly enceinte bride through the throng outside Newman United Methodist Church. "Dick Filips! Don't sneak off with the womenfolk. We need your signature."

"What's this about, boys?" Filips asked.

"We're recalling the sheriff. Berber problem's gotten out of hand."

"Berbers! Good Lord. Whole country's gone to the dogs. Did you read about that poor Indian feller in Oklahoma? Somebody tied him to a tree and horsewhipped him."

Nobody was sure how this related to Berbers, particularly inasmuch as the Indian probably was asking for it, but Filips was a football hero and allowed his foibles. He scribbled his name and walked on, holding the hand of his young bride. The hooded men sighed, scratched at the stains on their sheets.

Strangely, Mr. Voorhies himself refused to add his name to the petition as he left Newman United Methodist Church, merely looked at the men and walked on, shaking his head. On Monday a *Courier* editorial said the rape of the Frenchwomen was only a fiction story on the ladies' page;

besides, it had not happened here, but near Fez in Morocco, across the entire United States and beyond the Atlantic Ocean, in North Africa; and that the only Dark Skinned Fellows in Josephine County were the thirty-six remaining Rogue Indians who had not died during an influenza epidemic in 1914. If there was anyone to recall, it was the sheik who had done the kidnapping, but Local Voters did not have jurisdiction over a sheik. The recall fizzled out.

★   ★   ★

THERE WAS MUCH ABOUT THE EUROPEAN war, though it would be months before any of us had the chance to see action in defense of Democracy, if you did not count those fighting in Mexico or breaking for Canada to enlist on the side of His Majesty the King of England. In 1917 there was storming of barricades and hand-to-hand combat in Dobrudja and Romania, and Miss Edna Russ's mare foaled a two-headed mule which actually lived for a day. Dr. L.T. Davis made a pleasant call at the *Courier*'s office in town before heading home to Kerby, reporting that Mrs. Dick Filips in Ferrydale was expecting any day now. It was cold in January, and the year was only three days old when the American members of the joint Mexican Peace Commission were leaving the path clear for the American government to withdraw its troops from Mexico. In Petrograd it was cold, too, and the Russian government announced the capture of six hundred Teutons, three cannons and mine throwers, and a number of bombing mortars. Carl Bondarowicz's claim near Galice panned out, and, in addition to the regular program at the Rivoli, Edison's latest Wonder Talking Picture played, admission fifteen cents—ten if you sat in the balcony.

★   ★   ★

DAYS PASSED and there were reports of floggings and cross burnings and a man tied to a tractor with a gun held to his head, and still there was confusion as to whether martial law had been declared here or elsewhere, in Siam or Oklahoma or Abyssinia. Calling cards were printed at the *Courier*. On the streets there was much discussion. People stopped you with wild looks in their eyes and asked questions, and you responded as best you could.

"Is there an Extra edition?"

"Not that I heard of, Dick. How is Elizabeth taking all this news? Is she feeling all right?"

"As well as can be expected," Filips said. "How are we supposed to know what happened if there isn't an Extra? I heard the Duma has been forbidden to meet. The Imperial Guard has been called out."

"Probably there is a mistake. I don't think there is an Imperial Guard here."

"It was in the paper," Filips insisted.

"Mr. Voorhies will run a correction tomorrow."

"We are supposed to be indoors by sundown on penalty of death. They have orders to shoot on sight. People, cats, dogs."

"I don't see any soldiers."

"It's four-thirty, it'll be dark soon. My brother would think we're weaklings to put up with all this, the way he writes from Edmonton. He signed up, you know. I'm so ashamed. I can't. Wife expecting and everything."

"The street lamps are already on."

★   ★   ★

OUR NATION was neutral. It was still only January, though the snow had gone, and our sons were restless. A large shipment of Japanese tea-grass chairs had just been received from the Orient, at Helmer's, visitors welcome, and a number came, including the Dick Filipses of Ferrydale, seeking elegant and sturdy things with which to furnish the new house upon the arrival of Mr. Stork. Isaac Coy, of Gold Hill, was registered at the Grants Pass Hotel, on his way to visit an uncle in Portland. Germany promised Blaikie would not be shot. The residents of one ancient Italian city were said to have used no less than 340,000,000 gallons of water a day merely to bathe.

★   ★   ★

THE KAISER stormed French positions on Hill 304, and we found it fantastically funny to imagine the old moustachioed man (cousin or brother or some relative of His Majesty the British Monarch) scrambling through the barbed wire into the pop and rattle of rifle fire.

Still, the Kaiser looked more fit than Wilson, sorry to say, and he even wore uniforms sometimes, which President Wilson never did.

★   ★   ★

"HE'S HERE, SOMEONE SAID. The President! His train must've arrived overnight."

"I didn't hear of any train last night."

"He did! I saw his picture in the paper."

We rang the fire alarm, as few times as possible so as not to wake the President if he had slept in. We called out the volunteers and scrambled around getting the Grants Pass High School Marching Band together. Mayor J.P. Truax rushed over, reading to himself a quick proclamation he had scribbled on his laundry receipt. Then we rushed to the train station to greet President Wilson, while children and shopkeepers and women and Chinamen fell in behind us. But the station was empty except for Station Master Q.B. Rodale and his dog, which had just cornered a rat and shaken its head off. (Didn't he know that pest inspection estimates were available from Gowers at 7 N.E. G Street?) Rodale took off his green eyeshade and made gestures through the cage window and told us to clear out, we were tracking in mud. He said he had thought we were an invasion of Prussians at first, tramping in like that in our Navy blue band uniforms, and everyone laughed. If President Wilson were here, nobody told Rodale. Maybe the President had motored down from Roseburg and observed, unaware, all our activities, clubs, council meetings, and school bond issues. He was a sensitive man, and he felt our yearnings and fears and hopes, made note of them in a small journal he kept, and then told his driver to move along to another small town in a far part of America to learn about those people, too.

★   ★   ★

IT WAS CONFIRMED that there was no martial law in Grants Pass, and we flocked to the Star that evening and Monday only for Louise Huff and John Bowers and Lottie Pickford in "The Reward of Patience." Mr. Carl Filips made a visit in town to report that his elder son Luke—the thin one, you recall: acne problem, never much of an athlete like his brother—

had, amazingly enough, received kudos during training near Edmonton, while younger son Dick gallantly remained home to provide for the wife. An outnumbered Russian force, fighting in a dense snowstorm on a frozen marshland, recaptured the small island of Glaudon, north of Illuxt and south of Riga. The wire correspondent was nearly going deaf from the noise as he wrote. He could hear the screams of the soldiers, and smoke billowed even two miles away, and peasants smelled burnt powder in their tunics for miles down the road as they fled with their oxen and families.

★   ★   ★

ADMIRAL DEWEY was near death in Washington, and we were certain that he would have stopped the torpedoing of ships had he not been so ill. The *Courier* revealed what some of us called a Hun bias the day of Dewey's death when it ran a small headline, "Hero of Manila Bay passes away," under an enormous banner, "German raider sinks 23 merchant ships: Sea Wolf operating in the Atlantic creates greatest havoc in naval history." How could this happen, when the wire provided every item of information, factually and without flaw? How could Mr. Voorhies make such a mistake? Perhaps he had been out of town. Underlings can never be trusted in commerce, journalism, or the business of statecraft.

★   ★   ★

ANGEL CAKES were still available at 190 J Street, and some of us ordered them for birthdays and weddings.

★   ★   ★

THE REV. E. NATHAN BOOZER PREACHED a sermon at Bethany Presbyterian Church on the subject of "The Altar in a Pile of Rubbish," and a service for young people followed at seven o'clock that evening, at which a guest speaker, Sgt. Gerald Charing, gave a testimony certain to win the recalcitrant to religion, and a number of young men, including a group from Ferrydale, eagerly discussed matters concerning theology and service to their country after the talk. One of their number, N.R. Filips, read the scripture, and he was seen to have tears in his eyes for his older brother, now in Edmonton and soon to be shipped off in the service of Canada and other parts of the Free World, such as India and England and Rhodesia.

★   ★   ★

IN FEBRUARY WE stayed home and read or went out to see movies as they came to the Rivoli and Bijou and Joy. A number of gay young people, including Mr. and Mrs. N. Richard "Dick" Philips, G.W. Pearson, Amy Hanson, and Mr. and Mrs. Paul Sharon, even drove to Grants Pass to see the talked-about play, *A Bird of Paradise*, by Richard Walton Tully, author of *Omar the Tent Maker*. It was a love story of Hawaii and a play of a woman's soul, and we heard the Hawaiian singers and players and saw the wonderful volcano scene.

The next day there was a correction of the misspelling of a name, Mr. and Mrs. N.R. "Dick" Filips, it should have been, the *Courier* regretted the error. At the Bijou we saw, through the new Simplex machine, the stirring drama called *The Evil Women Do*, full of intrigue and retribution and vengeance. That year most ladies sighed in relief upon learning the Oregon Senate's decision that Oregon women could not serve on juries. Why should the weaker sex be drawn into the sordid details of drunken brawls, knifings over panned-out mining claims, and kidnappings by salacious Berbers?

★   ★   ★

THERE WAS SO much good news the first few months of that year, it was difficult not to become a silly optimist. General Douglas Haig reported in February that the British troops were gained to a depth of one thousand yards on a half-mile front on both sides of the Ancre toward Bapaume. One thousand yards! You can walk that in a few minutes, but no one is shooting at you. We were thrilled here at home to read that provisions for tourists would be offered at the mouth of the Oregon Caves, no doubt enticing tourists who would boost the Local Business Climate in the next few years. A new club formed Saturday afternoon to promote the caves, taking the name Oregon Cavemen. The men elected officers including Jim Stallworthy, Chief Big Horn; Abram Kittleman, Mammoth Slayer;

Mo Koloff, Witch Doctor; and Harrison Lacca, Treasurer and Activities Director. The men concluded the session by dressing in skins and parading through town with twigs and feathers in their hair, shaking clubs and clacking fossil rocks together.

★   ★   ★

MUCH AMUSEMENT was noted among bystanders.

★   ★   ★

THE VERY NEXT DAY we learned that Jimmy Stevens's "In Vaudeville" would perform at the Joy Theater, and that the German army of Crown Prince Rupprecht had received several sharp raps on the knuckles during the last six hours. Despite fogs and a thawing of the frozen ground and resultant seas of mud, the British raiders penetrated 250 yards into the German second-line trenches, and many dugouts were cleaned by gas. We did not fail to chew Wrigley's after every meal. The Commercial Club Minstrels offered the chance to see Grants Pass Society in Black Face and Specialty, and we wondered what specialties would be offered by those who might even include, for all we knew, Mr. Voorhies himself, wearing a top hat and doing a soft shoe. Alas, he did not even attend.

There was a scandalous picture of a woman cringing before a man with clenched fists, over a legend, "The Libertine." We sent a delegation to the *Courier* and demanded that Mr. Voorhies provide us the name of the brute, so that we could lynch him, but the publisher did not even come out to speak to us. He sent a copy boy with a note reading, "It was only a moving-picture ad."

We lynched the boy instead and went on home.

★   ★   ★

J. L. GREEN and family moved back on the farm again, as they had traded their town property off recently.

★   ★   ★

A BOY, Nathan Richard "Dick" Jr., 7 pounds 4 ounces, was born Tues. at 2 a.m. in Grants Pass Hospital to Mr. and Mrs. R.N. Filips.

★   ★   ★

MESSRS. B.F. BURLEY and R.L. Mayhew, trappers and prospectors from Horseshoe Bend, arrived in town Saturday, bringing in the skins of three wildcats, which they had killed right here in Josephine County.

★   ★   ★

IT WAS AN AMAZING YEAR. With the help of editor Wilford Allen, Mr. Voorhies demonstrated the leased wire for interested members of the Chamber of Commerce and the Women's Christian Temperance Union. The wire rattled away a few sentences—a battle position and the number of casualties, a town in Columbia, a statement from the secretary of the interior—while Mr. Voorhies took code. Then Mr. Allen dug out encyclopedias, almanacs, a history of the Napoleonic Wars, a 1906 *Congressional Record,* copies of *Ivanhoe* and *Ben Hur,* a register of Teutonic knights, the *Illustrated Book of Historical World Costumes,* an atlas with maps printed in pale pinks and limes and blues, whereupon the publisher rewrote the stories into comprehensive explanations of everything that had gone on anywhere. Whether or not he had been there, he understood. It was as if the mysteries of the world communicated themselves to him in hieroglyphs, and he transformed them into a sweeping whirl of information that the rest of us could barely keep up with and read in a day. He did this every day. "No," he modestly assured us. "Wilford and the boys usually do all this."

Mr. Voorhies included photos from distant places and funny cartoons from big-city papers. The cartoons showed consumers benefiting from price controls, and we knew that was true because of the bargains at Schallhorn's Grocery:

Friday Only

Flour	$1.75
Citrus, large	20¢
Pearline, large	20¢
2 lbs. Peanut Butter	25¢
Bottolene, medium size	$1.00

Thus we puzzled why things could be so fine here, while in New York people were rioting for bread. This happened in Russia, also, but that was where the Czar was filling palaces with rare majolica and marvelous paintings and gold cufflinks, and sending boys marching row by row to meet the Kaiser. It made you nervous to think, though: no bread. We turned to the fillers at the end of the stories instead, and we laughed and laughed until we felt better.

★ ★ ★

GREEN OF the *New York Evening Telegram* drew a cartoon of a snowy hill covered with crosses, hundreds of them, with wood grain painstakingly detailed. Nobody seemed to recall the next day what the caption said, but we were sure it had been moving nonetheless, and not a few of us set aside the paper that evening with tears running down our cheeks. War was so wrong. All those young boys.

★ ★ ★

DR. L.T. DAVIES AGREED to care for all the sick and disabled poor persons (except Chinamen) of said county when they may need medicine or medical attendance or treatment. The Turks too received what one might describe as several sharp raps on the knuckles, and you wondered how the stuffy tea-drinking British ever lost the Revolutionary War, the way they fought so tremendously the world over while the so-called Yanks trembled in self-imposed Isolationism. The Turks threw their artillery into the Tigris River, the same Tigris where the world began, and the Britons under General Maude put the Ottoman troops to rout. The British ran too, pausing only to shoot and thus knock the Turkish soldiers over, sending them tumbling, head over heels like acrobats, knocking their curly-toed shoes from their feet.

★ ★ ★

WE KNEW THE ENEMY was weakening, which is what made it so funny when we saw the cartoon of a fat German in a battered Prussian helmet with the spike bent, who stared through metal bars at a basket of sausages and fruit and especially bread, loaves of light rye and pumpernickel and baguettes and a nondescript squarish object that might well have been zucchini bread. The legend read, "The Way to His Heart Is Through His Stomach," and the German (the Kaiser, he was probably supposed to be) was saying, "Und now dey vouldt break mein heart yet." It was funny, but it made you wonder when the bread shortage would hit Grants Pass.

★   ★   ★

THE NEXT MORNING we were afraid. People stopped you and said, "Have you gotten your bread today?"

"Not yet, Dick."

"You'd better hurry."

"Is it getting hard to find?"

"They're running out everywhere. There won't be any food by nightfall."

By midmorning, retail shops were closed. Schools released the children to run wild at ten-thirty a.m. There was a rush on the banks. We used all our savings to buy all the bread we could find, thousands of loaves. Everywhere you saw husbands heading home like worker ants with enormous brown-paper parcels on their backs. Just in case, we made second and third trips, until all the stores began posting signs like the one in Schallhorn's window: NO MORE BREAD TODAY DON'T ASK BAKERS GONE HOME.

Our closets and spare bedrooms were filled with packages of bread, and our houses smelled warm and floury and unsettling: bread does not keep long. In a week would we be eating people who had dropped dead in the streets, whose skin was as pale as old flour? It was night, and the streets looked oily under the electric lamps. The *Courier* said troops were shooting looters on sight, somewhere close, we were sure it had been. We listened for shots. We gathered in parks and on street corners and heard angry speeches by Anarchists and Marxists and Socialist Revolutionaries, and when members of the Jaycees urged us to show caution, we booed them down and threw bottles and rocks. We unfurled banners and marched downtown to confront the County Commissioners, thousands of us, carrying candles and torches, streaming in from side streets and joining together on broad avenues, stopping trolley cars and singing nationalist hymns: farmers, workers, shoemakers, seamstresses, children, a patriarch holding a gold shepherd's staff and wearing a miter. We carried crosses and petitions, and chanted, "Give us our bread."

★   ★   ★

SOMEHOW IN THE WHIRLING confusion of this darkest night of the first year of the wire, we converged not on the new Courthouse but on the *Courier* building, beneath the lighted window of Mr. Voorhies's second-floor office. We could see him hunched over a stack of copy as he worked in his shirtsleeves, his homburg removed. He was eating crackers. We watched as his thin jaw worked dryly, too rapidly to be tasting his food. He picked up a pipe and lighted it. The window was open eight or ten inches; and when he exhaled, wisps of smoke slipped through the opening and rose like ghosts in the night, like the souls of those who had died of malnutrition, each wraith crying silently for vengeance. We began chanting the publisher's name like the words of an Old Slavonic liturgy: "Voor-hies! Voor-hies! Voor-hies!" Children cried, "Save us!" Young men prostrated themselves in the snow.

★   ★   ★

MR. VOORHIES started when he heard the noise, and he put his face close to the window, shielding his eyes with his hands as he peered out. We fell silent. A surgeon's mask of condensation formed on the glass in front of his mouth and nose. After a moment he stood, blocking the light, casting his terrible shadow across the rows of heads. "Oh!" the crowd gasped. Women fainted.

Mr. Voorhies stuck his pipe out of the window and tapped it on the ledge, and ash fluttered down and sprinkled our hats and shoulders. He slammed the window closed and went back to work.

★   ★   ★

FOR A MOMENT we stood in the cold. We looked at each other. Then we rolled our banners and went home.

The next day the stores were filled with bread, and Schallhorn's had a sign in its window, BREAD IS BACK OUR BAKER WORKED ALL NIGHT BY POPULAR DEMAND. Nobody bought any bread for a week.

★   ★   ★

GOOD OFTEN PAIRS ITSELF WITH EVIL, like a neat uniformed police-man handcuffed to a dangerous criminal. When an unarmed American Vessel was torpedoed, the story ran on the day that W.C. Long made a brief trip across county lines and returned with the promise of employ-ment at the Woodville School next fall. We may have learned that white slavers had dared to appeal to Wilson for pardon, but Mr. and Mrs. G.W. Salvo, of Eagle Point, spent a short time in the Ferrydale region for a first glimpse of their grandson, Dick Filips, Jr., and many stories were ex-changed until late in the night. Our nation still was not engaged in com-bat, except to the south, whence Pershing returned, and we argued angrily on either side of the question in Europe, even in the presence of loved ones, visiting parents from Eagle Point, for one, who grew red in the face and accused President Wilson of wanting war all along to encour-age sons-in-law in errant dreams of glory at the cost of their duties to wives and firstborn infants.

"I don't want to hear any more of this nonsense. You got a respon-sibility to your wife and son."

"The Huns are conquering the world and you're talking about a thing like that. They'll be in this county any day."

"Well, that's a d—d fine attitude, if you ask me. Let me finish, Ruth. I want to say this. If they are going to be here, you'd better be around to keep them from galloping in and sweeping off your wife and son like they did to those Frenchwomen. How'd you like little Dickie to be raised by those people?"

"Those were Berbers. That was Africa, it turned out."

"I don't give a rap. They're all foreigners. It could happen here."

★   ★   ★

THEN IT WAS MARCH 15, and a revolution in the Russian Empire suc-ceeded, and Absolutism was to be followed by a more Democratic rule and a closer cooperation with the Entente Alliance in its attempt to crush the Central Powers. Also that day we learned of new fashions, fashions no one here would have dreamed up if he were crazy, fashions that must have fallen from the sky or the birds: a fruity turban, a peaked straw hat, and, as in this case (there was a picture), one trimmed with a metal ribbon and fruit clusters of high luster. Elizabeth (Mrs. N.R.) Filips pretended she had such headgear, too, and drew many laughs Wednesday last at the Bethany Ladies Guild as she entered the room with a feather duster tucked into her hat.

We laughed and laughed at the funny things printed at the end of the stories, though this was not something to tell Mr. Voorhies about. "Fillers," he snorted. "Mush for those soft in the head. If we didn't have to print them to fill out the columns, we wouldn't." We didn't care. These were amazing times, and we wanted something to laugh at and take our minds off all the terrible news and death notices, and the leased wire considerately provided for even that need. The *Courier* printed jokes everywhere:

> A Mail Exchange
> "Going to town?" asked Sammas of Tomuel.
> "Yep."
> "Will you inquire of my mail?"
> "Nope."
> "Rather unneighborly of you," commented a friend.
> "Can't help that. Last time I did it I had to lug a grindstone out to his place."

That ran the day before the abdication of the Czar made Russia a Republic. Three of our boys took off for Canada that week to sign up there, and a week later the Wonder Store Co. announced a Mercantile Tragedy: Unrestricted Slaughter of One of the Finest Stocks of Men's Clothing, Furnishings, Hats & Shoes in Southern Oregon. Nigger-brown shoes were available at half price.

Meanwhile, in other tragedies, the Kaiser dealt the French a blow in a minor action at Verdun, costing an estimated 7,063 casualties.

★   ★   ★

WE FORMED A LOCAL ARMY and spent days searching the woods for the enemy. On Lower River Road several divisions ran into advance units of the Austro-Hungarian Army, and our boys dug in and fought for days, using rifles and mortars and mustard gas that drifted the wrong way and killed Justin Lodge's new purebred Limousin cattle. Fokkers and Sopwith Camels fought terrible air battles overhead. The wheels of supply wagons bogged down in the mud, and we shot a cat that was found devouring the face of a dead soldier. Every night, flares burst in the sky and illuminated lines of reinforcements from Jackson and Curry Counties, trudging toward the front.

★   ★   ★

THE BOOMING of cannons was audible as far away as Williams, where Mr. and Mrs. E.L. Lind, of Yreka, were staying in the Pay Dirt Hotel.

★   ★   ★

SUDDENLY ON the Western Redoubt the five-nines stopped dropping in the trenches, and for an instant there was a terrible silence. Then came the sound of enemy voices yelling as they charged across the field. We fought desperate bayonet sorties in thick smoke, and many men died in hand-to-hand combat. We sent wires begging Wilson to declare war, to get supplies and food, to send Pershing to help us. Some of our boys became poets and penned fearful condemnations of war before they were killed. Sheriff Bill Lewis arrested sixteen women on immorality charges, and he burnt the tents at the rear of the lines where the females were running a steam bath, massage, and currency exchange (marks, rubles, liras, dollars, francs). Wives set up field hospitals, tamponed wounds, tied tourniquets, amputated legs with handsaws. The casualties had run to 1,362.

★   ★   ★

BUT THAT AFTERNOON, the *Courier* reported in an exclusive copyrighted story that in fact our own divisions were fighting each other. Everyone stopped shooting and waved their newspapers back and forth to blow away the smoke. The air cleared, and officers scanned the horizon with binoculars. Mr. Voorhies was right. We threw down our arms, huzzahed and danced with each other in the mud. We crossed the lines and shook hands with the enemy. The boys helped roll up the barbed wire in Justin Lodge's fields, which were torn up by tank traps and land mines and trenches that ran seven feet deep.

★ ★ ★

MARCH PASSED, AND OUR DESTINY FOR BETTER or worse came to fruition like a funny new-style hat. On April 6 we learned that the United States was at war with Germany, now lined up with Entente Allies to crush German Imperialism and to stop the Kaiser in his waging of ruthless and barbarous warfare and sinking of U.S. shipping. Veterans of the Great Josephine County War signed up, those blind or missing limbs, of course, remaining home to sell pencils on street corners. Veterans of the Indian Wars held a march in support. Mrs. D. Filips was said to have organized the Bethany Ladies Guild to stitch numerous mittens for the boys in combat including her husband, Europe sounding so cold. We found Mr. Voorhies at his best with his editorial, "Kaiser Runs Amok," which opined that the Kaiser had never stood for this country in the late war upon Spain, and only our reputation as a peace-loving people had protected him after the incident at Manila Bay, still fresh in the minds of many. Now our might as a nation was roused.

★ ★ ★

WHAT DID THAT MEAN? People on the streets asked rambling, brilliant, obsequious questions of Mr. Voorhies, questions interwoven with statistics and road conditions and references to international security and changes in battle fronts and the ethical matter of whether a married man with a baby would perhaps be less likely to be sent into combat, and the great man tapped his silver-handled cane against the side of his shoe and pulled his gold watch on a chain from his pocket and returned it as the questioner, a young woman crying and carrying a child named only this year for his father, touched Mr. Voorhies's arm as if to beg just one more moment of his valuable time, until he finally interrupted and snapped, "It's all in the paper. Every blessed answer to what you are asking. I don't have a personal acquaintance with Woodrow Wilson or Kaiser Wilhelm, and I can't read the future any better than you. I only know what comes over the leased wire. Read the paper. Read the paper! Do you hear me? It's all there."

*   *   *

THAT WEEK, Gim Chung's Chinese Store took out an advertisement including a signed statement (witnessed by a notary public) from eight people living in Medford and Central Point, who had been healed of ailments including measles, cramps, carbuncles, tumors, caked breast, chills, sore throat, black lung, diphtheria, heart trouble, poor circulation, catarrh, rheumatism, gout, gid fever, private infections, & c. All of them explained that had they not availed themselves of the Chinaman's secret herbs, they surely would be dead today. Dr. Snooker denounced this as partaking of "the heathen cures of the Yellow Man."

*   *   *

THAT EVENING at the service for young people we prayed for the brave local boys who had fallen in the battle for freedom, remembering especially those from this congregation.

*   *   *

THE G.W. SALVOS, of Eagle Point, came to fetch their daughter, who had that day received a letter from a young Lt. Wesley Streets of Kansas City, Mo., stating that U.S. forces had advanced fifty yards and dislodged certain remains from a tangle of barbed wire and found this letter for Elizabeth Filips in the pocket. Our boys had been held back for a week due to the barbarous machine-gun fire of the enemy, wherefore much would the brave lad be missed and upheld as an example and hero for all our boys, memorial service at 9 on Thursday in the Methodist Church.

*   *   *

THE ROGUE HOTEL was booked up with a party of twenty spelunkers from Seattle, who were headed for new accommodations at the Oregon Caves. The Puget Sounders found themselves greeted at night by a bonfire and a group of Cave Men chanting in Pig Latin.

$\star$ $\star$ $\star$

ADRIAN DEE formally declared he no longer assumed responsibility for the debts of his wife, who ran off with an actor from a traveling theater troupe and writes from Kansas City that she is fine and would like her brown riding boots to be sent.

$\star$ $\star$ $\star$

VALIANT NICARAGUA declared war on Germany and Austria-Hungary, with Guatemala likely to follow suit.

$\star$ $\star$ $\star$

BRIDGE REPAIRS were set for 9 a.m. to noon on Tuesday next. Caution in proceeding was requested, and those of us who could limit our trips were requested to do so.

$\star$ $\star$ $\star$

THIS NEW TECHNOLOGY MEANT that the rush of events would continue to dizzy us for as long as we could foresee, and there was nothing to do when dazed by it all but read the fillers and laugh and resist the fear of being overwhelmed by Izmir and Bolivia and China and Berlin and other places that we could see on a dark horizon like jagged broken totems, bespeaking not only an oppressive and ever-present past, but also the prospect of impending and momentous and irrevocable change, very close and menacing, threatening to do us in.

$\star$ $\star$ $\star$

A Pessimist
Tommy—Dad, what is a pessimist?
Dad—A pessimist is a man who would rather read the death notices in a newspaper than the jokes.

INMATES

THERE WAS NO ANNOUNCEMENT; THE PRIEST SIMPLY APPEARED one day, peering out the windows and shambling about the old rectory, his new home, on the outskirts of Port George, a Northern California coastal town that has since become notorious for the bludgeoning death of an African-American prisoner who had thrown his feces at the guards. But in 1987 the town was still debating whether to endorse the construction of a supermaximum-level state prison out by the tidal mudflats, and the region was five years away from the boom that would draw Wal-Mart and Bi-Rite to town and fill Café 24 and Ideal Drugs with construction workers and architects and then wives of the guards and the battered, forgiving girlfriends of the inmates, women who stuffed the mailbags with perfumed letters and aspired only to pregnancy during conjugal visits. The mills were closing, the congregation was shrinking, and the assignment of this priest was taken in some quarters as an insult, an old gnome presiding over the death of a parish. Even Louise Shippen's Church/Scene profile of the new cleric in *The Daily Record-Searchlight* was lacking the breathless piety one usually found in her copy, whether the topic was lesbian Methodists or the former daytime television actress who was using crystals to channel the spirit of an ancient holy man. Ms. Shippen was interested in Eastern mysticism and seemed irritated by a priest who "lived for four years in Asia, but never found time to investigate its ancient spiritual heritage. 'Plenty to keep me busy in the parish,' he chimed."

For a year, since the retirement of Father Roy, St. Stephen's had prayed for a priest, and now in reply came this mild French-Canadian

Jesuit, Jules Lafon, with a face that made babies cry. There was no way to be polite about it. One could not put a finger on anything specifically abnormal; it was the combination of features that added up to something monstrous: his lower eyelids drooped, revealing bloodshot white and only the slit of a pupil, and he grimaced grotesquely when smiling; his nose had been broken, like a boxer's, and his cheeks were as hollow as the punt of a champagne bottle. Father Jules was gaunt and bent; and, despite his age, his gray hair had a henna tinge, as if he were dyeing it. It made you squirm to stare at him for the course of an hour-long mass, excluding the time his back was to the congregation (exposing a dented, bald pate) while he raised the Host and knelt and raised it again, and then turned to reveal a visage such as one might have discovered in a Victorian ward for the criminally insane. But he seemed a good man, and in the end one can grow accustomed to anything. At least, everyone thought, We've got a priest again.

The congregation had trouble getting a fix on him. Some priests like to hector you on subjects they know nothing about—marriage, for example, like some bachelor uncle who, angry at a young nephew's pleasure in the company of women, persists in warning his girlfriends about his intentions—but Father Jules was different; he seemed pained at having to offer the slightest reproof. This was good, perhaps, yet you sensed he repressed a great deal. It was January, and he slept in the rectory for a week before he mentioned to anyone that the heating was broken.

Father Jules rapidly settled in to his tasks. He baptized infants in their miniature wedding dresses, warbled mass in tones of utmost despair, limped around the yard planting garlic bulbs, thanked the ladies for the dinners they dropped off but was once seen to scrape an entire casserole into the garbage out back—he was that fussy about what he ate. He rambled in sermons quoting Sir Thomas More, Nelson Mandela, Randal Terry, Terry Anderson, Solzhenitsyn.

To everyone's surprise, the priest soon became friends with Tom Corcoran, algebra teacher, city councilman, and varsity basketball coach— and Corcoran, despite the Irish name, was not even a Catholic. They were the unlikeliest pair, the broken old priest and the youthful coach: divorced, affable, six-foot-six and a touch beefy, yet so handsome that he still, at thirty-nine, received love letters from girls who had hardly begun shaving the down from their legs. He was never quite able to denude the cleft in his chin of whiskers, so that it had a vaguely obscene quality, like the backside of a man in the shower. There was something Southern in his accent. You wanted him to like you. When he made his opinion known on the council, even those who had shown up to yell about, say, the proposed sewer bond issue, hastened to preface their criticism by lining up their views with his: "Well, I agree with what Tom said, but—"

The priest was a basketball fan, and he was seen at every Port George High School game. It was less widely known, however, that Lafon was a former high-school basketball coach himself, not to mention a center (and fullback, during football season) for the Jesuit college he had attended decades ago in Montreal. Around town, Corcoran said it was obvious that Lafon, who would have been tall had his spine not been so bent, had been injured on the field. The coach wasn't exactly sure how it had happened: a leap for a pass, a ferocious tackle, a late hit, a flying elbow in the days before helmets had face masks, a broken nose and crushed vertebra. In any case, Corcoran admired the priest's perseverance amid adversity. True, this virtue was also evident in the kid with cerebral palsy who lowed when he talked, puttered through the halls on what looked like a golf cart, and still managed to pull straight A's. But Corcoran found something tragic in an athlete struck in his prime by accident or illness—look at Lou Gehrig. Perseverance! For years he had been knocking this into the heads of the queers and wussies and women and geeks who tried out for his teams.

Corcoran had drafted the priest his first week in town for the pregame locker room prayer (this honor was rotated among the clergy, and there had not been a Roman Catholic for some time), but their friendship began in earnest the night the coach dropped by with a housewarming gift, a bottle of Kentucky bourbon. The priest offered Corcoran a drink, and the coach said, no, really, save it, you don't have to break it open tonight; but of course he did, especially when he learned that the coach had no one waiting at home. Lafon said this surprised him; despite the fulfillment he found in the service of God, his deepest burden was the loneliness, sitting alone in a restaurant with a plate of mussels and a glass of sauvignon blanc, while at the next table over sits a man with a wife of thirty years and five children and a grandchild or two, and they laugh and sample each other's dinners and engage in ordinary conversation about an idiotic employee or a kitchen that needs remodeling, interrupting themselves from time to time to admonish a child or admire a crayon camel scribbled on a placemat; at such times you see what you're missing. Plus you eat faster, Corcoran said. It's impossible to prolong your dinner for more than fifteen minutes when you're alone, and you feel ripped off if it's a nice restaurant and you've forked out twenty bucks, wine included. Precisely, the priest said. Which is why he was surprised a good-looking young fella like Corcoran was single. The coach found something sad in this man's acknowledgment of loneliness. He mentioned his divorce, then changed the subject to basketball.

They spent the evening talking—or rather, Corcoran talked, for the most part, he later recalled with embarrassment (he had not realized how starved for conversation he was), while Father Jules listened. For some reason, Corcoran went on about his son, Cody. The boy was a natural athlete, but he had never shown any interest in basketball until this season, the year of his parents' divorce, when he tried out for and made varsity, as if to hurl in his father's face some message Corcoran had yet to decipher. Suddenly the coach was ashamed of the intimate turn of the conversation. Do people always spill their guts while chatting with priests? he wondered. The guys must get sick of it. So he switched to his personal theory of mental preparedness. When Father Jules did vouchsafe an opinion, Corcoran was surprised at a nagging sense of his own ignorance and even fraud, as in a dream where one must land a 747 or conduct brain surgery. The coach was used to being heeded and respected. People sought his opinion, particularly on matters relating to his areas of expertise: sports, mathematics, juvenile delinquency, the tourism subcommittee, and the water/sewer issue in the urban growth boundary. But although he had a master's in education and doctorate in kinesiology, he was unable to grasp Father Jules's theory of sports science, which was derived from a fusion of John Wooden and Thomas Aquinas' doctrine of the prime mover. With his half-spectacles settled on his nose, the priest quoted *Summa Theologica*.

"Isn't that the entire science of the game: transforming the potency to act—and, of course, knowing when to strike?" Lafon said. "It's a beautiful thing to see a pass hurled into a crowd of defenders, and a center appears at that precise instant from nowhere and grabs the ball and flips it in—not dunks it: too crass; simply rolls it off the palm and the fingers, backwards."

"That's the part that's impossible to teach," Corcoran said. "Instinct."

"Don't get me wrong: I'm not saying your boys should read Thomas to bone up on strategy," the priest added, and Corcoran wondered if the priest was pulling his leg.

"We're only up to Augustine," he said, and Lafon laughed.

"Drills," he went on, more to himself than the coach. "I always loved watching the drills. Three boys weaving down the court, firing the ball back and forth, never dribbling, never traveling. Or when offense passes around the key, and the entire defense shifts with the ball, as if it were a field of gravity. That for me always had the satisfaction of a mathematical equation."

"That's one thing basketball never reminds me of: math," the coach said. "And I teach it."

— The priest was helpless at the little repairs that had to be done at the rectory, and Corcoran took on projects there, hanging a curtain, repairing a toilet that flushed on its own every few minutes as if a ghost were hitting the handle. When he learned that a moving van would be dropping off Lafon's books and other personal articles, Corcoran rounded up a work detail, which annoyed church members who would have been happy to help.

For starters he drafted his son. Cody was a sixteen-year-old with frizzy hair like a mushroom; despite a slight stammer, he was a show-off, a clown, popular with the girls because of his prowess in three sports. Admirers egged him on. Without an audience, Cody never would have stolen the hood ornaments from sixteen Mercedes at Jim's Classic Foreign Autos last year, or tried to pull down the Grants Pass caveman statue with Corcoran's own pickup after that school's homecoming game last November. Cody lived with his mother, and the boy's eyes still flashed with the anguish and affront that had come over him the day his parents sat him down and said they couldn't go on like this anymore. At practice Corcoran sometimes caught Cody staring at him; on weekends, when the boy stayed with his father, they saw little of each other, for Cody was always out with his friends. But with his son present, Corcoran could count on enough help to unload whatever a priest accumulates over a lifetime.

There was too much help, really. Corcoran and two kids cleared out the minivan (not a moving van, it turned out) while Cody and another boy screwed around. The priest wandered about in an abstracted state, opening boxes randomly, rediscovering lost books, thumbing through a history of the Lakers, which he tried to discuss with Corcoran just as the coach was hefting a box containing a multiple-volume work on the Tridentine Mass. Having doffed his clerical garb for the day, Lafon cut a ridiculous figure in sandals, dark socks, a Hawaiian shirt, a sweater he must have found at a St. Vincent de Paul, and pants as absurdly baggy as a skateboarders'.

When Corcoran tried to move a bookcase, the priest, suddenly efficient, lurched forward to help. "That's okay, Father," Corcoran said. "We'll take care of it. Zawacki! Make yourself useful." Kyle Zawacki grabbed the other end of the bookcase, and they carried it toward the living-room wall. The boy was the best player Corcoran had ever coached, but he had been arrested last summer for slamming his twenty-year-old girlfriend into a wall until she lost consciousness. The jury acquitted him, though. He had scored thirty-three points in the state quarterfinals that year. Suddenly, Zawacki guffawed and dropped his end of the bookcase.

"Hey! You nearly threw my back out," Corcoran said. "Pay attention."

"Sorry, coach."

But as soon as they lifted the bookcase, Zawacki started snickering again.

"What's with you?" Corcoran asked.

"Nothing. Cody is just being a dork."

"Cody, don't be a dork. And don't say 'dork' around a man of the cloth, Zawacki, you'll make his ears burn."

Corcoran turned to wink at the priest. What he saw was this: Lafon ambling across the room, reading, while Cody, bent double like a hunchback, gimped along behind in imitation. The boy ogled his friends with a bug-eyed, hunchbacked expression, and they snorted, wept, suffocated their laughter.

"Cody!" the coach said. Lafon glanced back and saw the boy. Agonizingly, the priest registered no anger. He ducked into the study with a pained expression. "You!" Corcoran said, grabbing Cody by the arm. "Outside!"

In the front yard the coach demanded, "What the hell were you doing?"

"What do you mean?"

"You know what. Give me forty burpies."

"Dad, I was only kidding."

"Fifty. One more word and you're grounded this weekend."

Cody dropped on the frosty lawn and launched into his burpies: down, two, three, one. Down, two, three, two— He did not take his eyes off his father.

"I am so pissed I can hardly speak," said Corcoran. "What were you trying to prove, gimping around like that? How would you like it if I joked about—"

Cody's eyes widened in anticipation of a jab at one of his shortcomings (his stammer, his inability to master even the simplest mathematics equation), and Corcoran felt a pang and cut himself off. He had a sudden awareness of how much pain his divorce had inflicted, of his utter failure not only as a father but even at the modest goal he had declared when Cody was born—to always be his son's friend—and the thought was too much to consider right now. He broke a switch from a crab-apple tree and whacked the trunk seven times. Down, two, three, thirty-one. Down, two, three, thirty-two. Suddenly he felt like a slave driver and threw the switch on the roof.

When Cody was finished, he blurted out, as if to justify himself, "You keep acting like Father Lafon's some big football hero. Well, he's not, he's just an ex-con. His back was broken in prison, that's why he's all hunched over."

"That's bullshit. Who told you that?"

"Zawacki's dad heard it from a priest who stayed at their motel."

"Zawacki's dad? Oh, right. Chip Zawacki was probably stoned at the time. If Father Jules was ever in prison, he was a chaplain. They wouldn't let him be a priest if he was an ex-con. It's like with teachers."

"I swear to God, that's what he said."

"So what was Father Jules supposedly in for?"

"Something about being a Communist."

"Son, I've got news for you: Communists are atheists."

"Thank you, Dad, I appreciate that information." Cody added, "Maybe it's a lie. Why don't you ask him?"

"You know, I'm really not interested in this discussion. What interests me is seeing you apologize for being such a jerk."

They returned to find the old man dusting a battered leatherbound Erasmus on his shirt. As Cody spoke, his stammer became so pronounced he could barely get the words out: "Father Jules, I'm sorry. I didn't mean anything."

The priest licked his finger and scrubbed at a spot. His ears had turned scarlet, but otherwise he showed no embarrassment. "That's all right, my son." Then he smiled grotesquely. "You know, Cody, I wasn't always like this."

▬ The next day it snowed, swirls of white that scumbled the redwoods across the valley and drifted in particulate eddies in the middle distance of the courtyard. The snow splotched his hair and dark woolen coat like spatters of plaster. For the first time he could remember in eight months, Corcoran was happy. Trotting up the stairs to the gym, with its brick-and-stucco facade and barrel roof jumbled with chimneys and air conditioners, he glanced at the humanities building, where a skeleton hung in a third-story window of an art class. Lately the skeleton had seemed a grim reminder of mortality, but today someone had placed a red derby on its head, rendering the collection of bones no more fearsome than a Halloween costume.

Inside, somebody had cut the lights after seventh period P.E., and the coach groped through the lobby and stumbled around in the dark gym until he found the switch. The lights came buzzing on gradually, so that the room proceeded from night to day in a continuum of imperceptible degrees, as a full moon is given birth by a dark horizon. Corcoran swung his whistle by its string around his finger and surveyed the old gym where he had spent every winter afternoon for nine years. The place was redolent of old wood and varnish and dusty heating vents and the acrid sweat of adolescents. Above the stage hung posters from rallies ("SASQUATCHES—JUST DO IT") and pennants from conference championships as ancient as 1922. The varsity now played in the new gym, and this building was relegated to P.E., practice, and J.V. games.

Corcoran wheeled out a cart full of leather basketballs and palmed one—rhino-skinned, hyperinflated, brown with sweat and dirt. It had a delicious fullness in his hands. Dribble: the ball springs from the floor. Corcoran hooked a shot from the top of the key. The ball swished through the net and bounded back to him. He fired from the corner, and the ball ricocheted violently inside the rim and went down for three. The players began drifting in after a three-mile run, varsity in red, J.V. in white with the word "DEFENSE" across the butt, and Corcoran returned his ball to the cage, for it was unseemly for a coach to be caught shooting a basket.

He blew his whistle and hollered, "All right, all right, gentlemen. Bleachers. Let's go. We ain't got all day."

The boys ran the bleachers while dribbling balls, up one row and down the next, making sure to hit every step from row A to ZZ. In a game the basketball bounces with a singular thud, but in practice, with twenty balls concurrently thumping, there is no individual drumbeat: the whole gym rumbles as if in an earthquake.

When the boys finished their laps, Corcoran had them run a great circle around the court. Each kid jump-shot, grabbed his rebound, dribbled pell-mell for the other basket, shot again. Corcoran and Tim Harris, the assistant coach, stood under each basket with their forearms wrapped in foam-rubber pads. As each player drove in for the shot, a coach gave him a shove to simulate the rough-and-tumble of a game.

Horton, Glazier, Zawacki, Pennington, Van Der Heuvel, Mann— the boys came at Corcoran, one flushed face after another, biting their lips when they set up to shoot. They had lost the intensity of the first days of the season, when they still believed Corcoran could harangue and exhort a championship out of them, and still feared his wrath should they fall short. Now they were 10-7, with three straight losses, and, surveying the schedule ahead, it was conceivable they would not win another game this season.

■ Corcoran bumped McDonough, who came down on the coach's foot. "Shit!" they both said. Corcoran thumped McDonough on the back of the head. "Sorry, Coach," the boy said.

At the far end of the court, Cody was showing off, feinting right and going left around Harris. He spun the ball behind his back and dunked it. Harris (idiot!) didn't rebuke Cody, and so the other boys followed suit, with smart-ass dribbling and Globetrotter lay-ups, and the drill fell apart.

"Gentlemen, I want to see a base-line jumper," Corcoran shouted, but the kids at the other end of the court chose not to hear. And Corcoran had to concentrate on the boys coming at him: De Boer, a debate team member whose dad sold Japanese cars. Marks, who covered junior high sports as a stringer for the *Record-Searchlight*. Adams, who already had a drunk-driving record. Kremicki, who could swear in Spanish after a summer bossing a crew of Mexican tree planters.

Corcoran harassed and thumped each kid. They barely tried. At sixteen or seventeen, boys should not be so resigned. At thirty-nine a coach should not let them get away with it.

Humphrey, Knox, Pedersen, Cox. Dingell, Dowell, Drager, Knox. Corcoran. Who drove straight for his dad with a glower that recalled Zawacki the day he was arrested on the assault-and-battery charge. At the last minute, Cody feinted right and whirled left. It was a fine move, and all Corcoran could do was foul the boy as he went up to shoot: he shoved him, hard. Cody managed to release the ball as he crashed to the floor. Corcoran heard the net swish behind him.

He blew his whistle and stopped the drill. "I want a base-line jumper. I don't want a goddamned hook or a lay-up. Now, Cody, get off your ass and get moving."

For a moment, Corcoran was afraid that Cody, groaning on the floor and clutching his knee, was seriously hurt. But the boy stood and limped toward the door, holding the ball against his hip.

"Cody!" Corcoran said. He wanted to ask, Are you okay? But that couldn't be done, not in practice, not in the face of such defiance. So he said, "You walk out, you're out of here for good."

For a moment, Corcoran thought Cody would throw the ball at him. Instead he drop-kicked it into the bleachers and limped out of the gym. At the door on his way out he slugged the wall. The kids watched Corcoran.

"All right, gentlemen, let's go," he shouted, and the rumble of dribbling resumed.

Corcoran noticed a dark figure hunched in the bleachers with his chin on his palm. "Excuse me!" he shouted. "Practice is closed." Then he realized it was Lafon, who compounded Corcoran's embarrassment by waving broadly as if from the far side of the fairgrounds. He hobbled down the bleachers.

"Oh, Father Jules, I'm sorry, I didn't recognize you. You don't have to go."

"Rules are rules."

Glazier came dribbling at the coach, and Corcoran tore his attention from the priest and bumped the boy.

It was dark when he left the gym, and Cody was nowhere to be seen. The snow had stopped, and in the courtyard the slush was trampled and muddy. The lights were still on in a third-story window of the humanities building, where the skeleton dangled by its chain, like the remains of a traitor hung from the city gates. From his office he phoned Cody at his mother's. "He came home crying," Karen said. "I hope you're proud of yourself." She hung up.

That night, Corcoran dropped by the rectory with another bottle of bourbon. He felt the need to justify his outburst with Cody, but when he pulled up, he suddenly grew angry—why the hell did he owe Lafon an explanation?—and he remained in his car, wringing the paper bag around the bottle's neck. The rectory was dark except for the study, where the priest sat at a desk by a curtainless window. In this light his expression was distorted and the hollows in his cheeks were exaggerated, like a face in a photograph of prisoners of war. The thought brought a stab of sadness.

Sighing, he got out, stuck the bottle in his coat pocket, and nudged the car door closed with his hip. At the sound, the priest looked up. The anonymity vanished; he had reassumed his own elegiac ugliness.

Lafon was not surprised to see Corcoran, but he blushed as he accepted the bourbon, as though embarrassed at the implication that he needed to be kept in booze. And anyway, they skipped the bourbon and drank Rob Roys, a favorite of Lafon's, in his study, surrounded by old volumes in Latin, Hebrew, Koine, Attic, Chinese. For bookends the priest used small sculptures he had acquired in Asia: teak elephants and tigers, a miniature ivory Taj Mahal, a metal scribe with a wise and bemused countenance, and a porcelain Buddha such as one might see in a Vietnamese immigrant's doughnut shop, with a cinnamon twist and a cup of coffee and a garland of flowers laid out in offering before it. The priest moved to a couch and tucked an orthopedic pillow in the small of his back.

Corcoran flipped a chair around backward and perched on it. Abstractedly he swirled the cherry in his martini glass; finally realizing he had not tasted his drink, Corcoran sniffed the liquor and threw down a gulp. His face contorted with the expression of a cat coughing up a hairball. "The hell's this, airplane fuel?" he asked. The priest assented, then inquired about the team. Corcoran understood this as an invitation to talk about Cody, and he produced from his wallet a sixth-grade school picture which he had carried for five years—the babyish face, the eagerness, the Disneyland T-shirt that was later torn up when Cody fell off a horse and landed in a blackberry bush.

"He's almost grown up," the priest said, and returned the photograph.

"I hate it when that happens. You know, he was such a sweet little guy; now all I see is this anger, this brooding. Jules, it's the most terrible thing to have your son turn on you. I deserve it. I was unfaithful; I'm sure you figured that out" (though from the look on his face, the priest had not). "And because Karen and I no longer loved each other, maybe I wanted her to find out. But Cody had no idea, he never saw the divorce coming. Whenever he looks at me, I see these accusing eyes."

He had never expressed such sentiments to anyone, and he blushed. Abruptly, Corcoran asked, "So how long were you there? At practice, I mean."

"Fifteen minutes. I don't know."

"Not your most Thomistic drill today."

"Room for improvement."

"I'm not usually like that—well, okay, I'm always like that, in terms of yelling when I get torqued; you know that from watching me at games. But I don't normally knock my kids around."

"That was quite a shove you gave him."

"I guess I was still teed off about the other day when he started following you around." The coach cut himself off. The priest was not fooled, and was possibly offended, by the implication that Corcoran pushed Cody in retaliation for the boy's mimicry. "Well, it wasn't that. It's just, I'm a jerk sometimes. I can't stand kids who defy me to my face, and my own son—. I used to think you can mold character, but now I believe my influence is negligible. Even with my boy. Especially. I wish he'd never tried out for the team."

"He knows you think that."

"You talked to him?"

"I found him in the hallway slugging the wall. (I've always wondered why jocks do that.) He said he wanted to play basketball because he was afraid you would forget him after the divorce."

"Then how come he's so damned defiant about it? He told you that?"

The priest nodded. For a moment the men drank in silence.

Finally the coach ventured, "Jules, I know this is stupid, but I thought you should know there's this rumor going round. Actually, it was Cody who heard it, so consider the source—but he said that you were in prison. I told him it was ridiculous, but he claims to have heard it in town."

The priest drained his glass, rose painfully, and retreated into the kitchen, and Corcoran was faced with the horrifying realization that in addition to being a lousy husband and a father, he had now behaved like the worst sort of small-town gossip and passed on hurtful nonsense under the guise of friendship. Lafon did not return. Apparently, Corcoran was supposed to leave now. But just as he stood up to go, the priest came back with a tray bearing bottles of scotch and dry vermouth, and a jar of maraschino cherries. He mixed them each a second Rob Roy and began talking about his coaching days, when he was a missionary in China. Corcoran had always imagined Lafon at a school in Pittsburgh or Buffalo, coaching a small but tough team of Irishmen and Italians and Croatians and perhaps even blacks in the days before schools were supposed to have been integrated; he was disappointed to learn it was a mission school in Harbin, four decades ago.

Chinese basketball players! It sounded like a joke. But Lafon insisted his teams were not bad, at least not under the circumstances. His best kid had been a center named Tseng.

■ *He was not a good player* [Lafon said] *in the way you think of it: a skilled athlete. He was just huge, for China, anyway: six-five: one of those giants who dominate the sport in their own country, but when they play in the West, they are merely average, and terribly clumsy, I might add, and everyone runs circles around them. Our game strategy was simple: you just lobbed the ball down court to Tseng, and he shot and bounced it off the backboard two or three times, always rebounding over the heads of the others, until the ball went in. But he made up for that in his determination in school; he was a great student, a wonderful boy. Parents were converts.*

This was 1950, not long after the Reds seized power, and I was keeping my head low: saying Mass, teaching, coaching. They were already expelling foreign mis-

sionaries, but when the Korean War broke out, everything went to hell. The government's hostility increased, old friends didn't recognize you on the streets, and I now knew firsthand of doctors, priests, and teachers who had disappeared. The Russians were already pulling out—before the Japanese occupation, there had been a hundred thousand of them in town, and the city had a dozen onion-domed churches, some of them truly beautiful. Anyway, the people who would talk to me said I should leave while I could, but I loved China, and I somehow believed that love would spare me; the same hubris and naiveté was manifested by those Americans and Europeans who stayed on in Beirut until they became hostages—professor-converts to Islam, spouses of Muslims, reporters who thought the subtleties of journalistic objectivity would be appreciated by people who do not hesitate to blow up children, all believing themselves to be immune to the hatred of the West. But sometimes at night, I dreaded what might happen: I tossed and turned in bed as the wind blew down out of Siberia, and started awake whenever a branch rapped the windows or the dog barked.

The police came during a blizzard. They beat me and ransacked the school and tore apart the rectory walls with crowbars—looking for hidden radios or propaganda tracts—and after a cursory questioning I was jailed in a cell with eight other inmates, each more politically advanced than I, particularly the cell chief, who painstakingly explained, as if to an idiot, that it would be best if I searched my heart and immediately confessed everything.

"You were a prisoner in China?" Corcoran exclaimed, but the priest shook his head and raised his bony hands to deflect any admiration, and cried, "Wait. Wait; hear me out."

The formal interrogation took place in a room that smelled like a slaughterhouse and had an asphalt floor with a drain in the center. I remember wondering, as I stood with my head bowed respectfully, about the drain, and only after I was beaten did I understand: as I was dragged away another prisoner came in and mopped my blood down the hole. At a table my inquisitor sat, a judge with the profound gaze of the ascetic, the insane. He was a former dockworker, and his teeth were broken and jagged like a shark's, the result of a beating by Nationalist soldiers—so he told me bitterly, as if I had been a party to this crime.

There was also a stenographer, a handful of guards, and a chalkboard, on which a guard would occasionally write things I said. I could not understand why certain phrases were chosen. It did not make any sense.

"Let me outline the facts of the case," the judge said. "We know you have had extensive spy contacts with the imperialists dating back to the war. We have *evidence of perverse activities you have engaged in. We have proof your so-called basketball team was in fact an espionage organization for the purpose of sabotage, corrupting youth, and teaching counterrevolutionary values."*

"This is absurd," I said. "I was arrested because I am a priest; I thought China still allowed freedom of religion. This is persecution."

"You're only partly right: yes, in China there is freedom of religion. Therefore, what is occurring tonight cannot be persecution. You must be guilty of something. Our conversations will guide us to the answer to this question: Guilty of what? So tell me."

When I would not cooperate, he ordered the guards to handcuff my hands in front of me and jam a pole through my elbows behind my back. They beat me unconscious, roused me with water, beat me again.

At some point I was dragged back to my cell. The other prisoners took shifts keeping me awake, pinching and slapping me whenever I dozed off, demanding to know what it was that I was withholding. I believe I did not sleep for two weeks, although my mind was too confused to make any sense of those weeks. I was hallucinating, I was having conversations with my boys and my older brother and the Blessed Virgin herself.

You must understand that at this time you become so confused and desperate for sleep, you wrack your brains trying to understand what it is they are asking you, and how you can answer it without compromising yourself or injuring others. All have sinned and fallen short of the glory of God. Is it too much to admit this? No. I have always believed I am a sinner—a traitor, if you will—before God and man.

And that is the first step. For man is a guilty creature, and in such conditions you draw up mental ledgers of deeds you at some level regret. And the very formation of such ledgers opens a crack through which they will eventually gain access to your reservoirs of shame and guilt: guilt for your petty failures and great transgressions; for losing your temper with a student who subsequently never returned to school; for the fact that you, a servant of Christ, employed a servant of your own at the rate of a few cents a day (oh, they were good; they quoted Matthew 20:26–27 to me, and I began sobbing; I was a broken man by then). Guilt real and imagined.

The priest buried his face in his talons, and Corcoran thought he would cry, but he emerged and said flatly, "It's not so hard to get to a man."

Suffice it to say, I started by confessing to something that I thought would not implicate my boys: I said I forced them, against their will, to listen to the anti-Communist radio broadcasts of a certain Dutch priest. This was unbelievably stupid of me. I didn't know that this now rendered them, too, in need of "thought reform." The judge—I always had the impression he was snapping at an insect with his broken teeth when he shouted at me—showed me a photograph of myself with Tseng and his parents.

"You know this boy?" he asked.

I said, "I think he was in seminary with me." (My mind was going, you see.)

"He was one of your basketball players."

"Oh, yes. You're right, of course."

"Do you remember his name?"

"I don't know."

"This is Tseng. You remember him? He has been arrested."

Suddenly everything about the boy returned—his large hands, the lisping way he spoke Latin—and I cried. He continued, "We know he was working with you to supply information to the CIA."

I was confused. It did not make sense. "Tseng?" I said. "I'm sure you're wrong, I don't think he would do this."

"Don't lie to my face!" the judge exploded.

"I don't remember. For heaven's sake, I just don't remember."

"Then we will help you."

The judge ordered the guards to bind me. They laid me face-down with my mouth open on a concrete block and kicked the back of my head. That's how I lost my teeth. They nearly drowned me in a tub, revived me, drowned me again. I can't tell you how water terrifies me. They broke my collarbone, cracked my sternum and two ribs, stomped on me until I passed out. A medical officer would give me injections so that I would be conscious to feel everything. They fractured my hip and my back, so I later learned from the X-rays they took in Hong Kong after I was released. Apparently I'm lucky I can walk. They beat my body into what you see now.

To make a long story short, I was "reformed." Everyone is, to one degree or another—even the heroes—though perhaps not as shamefully as I. One day I talked so rapidly, the stenographer had to slow me down.

They were particularly keen on radios, so I confessed to making secret transmissions for the Vatican.

I said my life's work had been spying for British intelligence.

I admitted to all kinds of perversion with nuns, with prostitutes, with children.

The judge asked me to write a letter to each of my players, confessing I had been a Western spy all along and the purpose of basketball had been to instill in them capitalistic values of competition. That letter still pains me. I knew it would be used in their interrogations, should they be arrested, or simply to discredit me in their eyes; but at the time I believed it was true.

From then on, my treatment became milder, and they even had a doctor examine me with the intent of healing and not extending and intensifying the duration of my pain. The interrogations continued, but in place of the brutish judge was a missionary-educated man, a former candidate for the priesthood, who assumed the air of a schoolmaster who has your interests at heart and has infinite patience for this lesson. I was put in a new cell full of reformed missionaries, and we engaged in discussions on the purification of one's mind from bourgeois sentiments. You need to understand, we weren't pretending. I passionately believed in the historical dialectic, and yet somehow, I never ceased believing in Christ. Consciously this made sense to me, as it somehow does to Liberation Theologians. But my unconscious mind rebelled against it; panic attacks awoke me at night, and I prayed to Mary and meditated on her purity in contrast to my sins, until I finally slept.

We counseled other prisoners to our level of understanding. And so one day I was sent to talk to a man in solitary. When they opened the cell door, he lay in the fetal position on the floor, a small, naked man, like an overgrown Somali baby: all skin and bones, except for his bloated hands, which had been crushed.

His face, in profile, was puffy and unrecognizable. As I approached him, I realized his shortness had been an optical illusion of the cell. He was remarkably tall. It was Tseng. They were starving him to death.

As I began talking, he regarded me with anguish, and only as I saw myself in his eyes did I realize how thoroughly I had fallen. I wanted to ask his forgiveness. But I didn't. I didn't. I felt myself stepping back from emotion, into a state of tranquility, and I lectured him on the sin of pride.

He cut me off: "I never believed that letter until I saw you; I thought it was a forgery."

"My son, you must understand the futility of one man standing against history."

"Father, go away," he said.

"I'll pray for you—pray for courage."

I meant it, but he said, "How dare you talk to me about prayer!"

I was too ashamed to reply.

"Get out of here, please, stop poisoning me—you don't know how hard it is already."

I returned to the hall and talked with the guard so that I would not think or feel that which was forbidden. He could see I was upset.

"Don't worry," he said by way of comforting me. "He'll die soon."

The most severe manifestations of brainwashing lasted only a year or so after I had gotten out to Hong Kong. But in a subtle way, I suppose it still is there now; the strongest sense of all is guilt that I wasn't able to resist, that I had betrayed God and my people and my boys. And the knowledge of how frail selfhood is.

■ The next morning, Corcoran drummingly recalled the night, in bursts of stuffy, dry-mouthed self-castigation, damning himself for his initial awkward silence when the priest had finished, for his idiotic joke about how half his own team was probably going to end up in prison, for offering further details about his affair, not excluding the herpes (Christ! to a priest!), for his inability to offer any assurance of pardon beyond a meaningless assertion that "nobody could blame you, Jules." Beyond that, the night, considered now, from his bed the next morning, was a blank. Apparently he had drunk more after he got home—four beer cans were crushed beside his bed. When, after vomiting, he slumped to the kitchen and opened the refrigerator looking for mineral water, he discovered his wallet, his keys, and a great quantity of pennies and nickels and paper clips in the butter compartment. His inability to remember how or why these articles had ended up on a shelf by the orange juice made him rage at himself again. What if you'd killed somebody driving home in that condition?

Corcoran avoided Lafon for a week. At first this was intentional; he needed distance, and because he did not hear from Lafon he supposed the priest felt the same.

Eventually, however, he dropped by the rectory, after practice one Tuesday, then again on a Sunday afternoon. No one answered his knock. On the second occasion, Corcoran slipped under the door a note on a subscription card that had fallen from a *Sports Illustrated* in his car: "Hey, Lafon, we're losing without our good-luck priest. What are you up to these days?—TC" (The priest would understand the attempt at a joke: they had been losing even when he was attending the games.)

It was a time of solitude and estrangement for Corcoran, especially from his son. The first weekend, Cody was sick and remained at his mother's; the next, he said he was thinking about going skiing at Mount Bachelor with some friends. One day after school, Corcoran spotted Cody crossing the courtyard, and he called him inside the old gym. The lights were again out, and as the coach groped around the walls ("You'd think I'd be able to find the switch after all these years"), he heard a sigh: Sheesh. Forget the lights, Corcoran thought, and in the shadowy foyer with the boy side-lighted through the window by an overcast day, he launched into the speech he had been mulling over for the last two weeks. Corcoran had intended to apologize. But speeches never work, reconciliation is impossible, and the only direction we move is apart. Cody was sullen. And as they talked, the coach felt a pain in his stomach, a physical sense that discipline and authority, the only material he possessed for building a winning team out of small-town mediocrities, were slipping from his grasp. There are reasons for drills, he was saying; they draw a team together into something greater than the sum of its parts, something that functions with a mathematical precision—

"If you're trying to talk me into joining the team again, you're wasting your breath," Cody said.

"I'm trying to tell you, you won't get anywhere in life if you act like a butthead."

Cody walked out. Now it was Corcoran who felt like slugging the wall.

But that Sunday morning he was sleeping in when the phone rang. He knocked the receiver from the bedside table, groped around groggily, and said "What?" not hello.

"Dad?"

"Cody! Hey, you woke me up, dude. What's happening?"

"I'm at St. Stephens," and before Corcoran could voice his amazement, the boy added, "Father Jules isn't here yet."

"Well, it's only, God, Cody, it's not even 8:30. Most churches start at 10 or 11, don't they?"

"The early mass starts at 8, and nobody's seen Father. I was afraid something happened to him."

When Corcoran arrived, a clutch of parishioners had gathered in front of the church, watching a pair of old men knock at the rectory next door. Cody was standing on a planter as he peered in a window. Corcoran strode over in the sweats he had slept in and a Sasquatches warmup jacket. Catching a glimpse of his father, Cody rolled his eyes—whether at Corcoran's appearance or at the old men's incompetence, it was unclear; but Corcoran also detected in the boy's eyes an appeal for help.

"Are you the locksmith?" one old man said. "Oh, Coach, I should've known you. I doubt Father has gone far: the car's still here. This young fella here checked the garage."

Corcoran tried the front doorknob. It turned, but the chain was latched. "Jules?" he called. He glanced at the others, who shrugged. He shouldered the door in.

On the floor of the study they found the priest. He had collapsed while praying, it appeared, for he lay on his side next to a kneeling rail, clutching a rosary, his knees pulled to his chest. "Oh, my God," Cody cried. The old men crossed themselves.

— Corcoran felt Lafon's pulse at the throat. Then he gathered the bony priest in his arms and shoved through the crowd that had followed him into the rectory. "We'll take him to Harbor View. Cody, get the keys out of my pocket. You're driving."

Corcoran lay Lafon on the back seat of the pickup, then joined him in back and cradled the priest's head.

"And don't get us killed on the way," he said when the boy nearly backed into a log truck roaring down the highway.

Cody was florid, and he was jutting his jaw as Corcoran himself did when he was angry.

"You okay?" Corcoran said.

The boy nodded.

"How long you been going to church?"

"Couple of weeks." He ground the gears as he worked the shift. "It's something to do."

At the emergency room the nurses undressed the unconscious priest, and the coach was shocked at the scarred, emaciated body: rib cage, bony limbs, swollen belly. The nurses slipped on a hospital gown, carelessly exposing his shriveled genitals, which were missing a testicle. They took his pulse and blood pressure, attached an IV, fastened on an oxygen mask, hooked him up to a computer that monitored pulse and blood pressure.

The coach took Lafon's hand. Just then a doctor parted the curtain, nodded at the Corcorans, washed his hands as the nurse gave a report, and examined the patient. After a few minutes he turned to Corcoran.

"How long has he been like this?"

"I think he said since the 1950s. He was injured in a football game."

The doctor started to say something. Then he shook his head and went on with his examination—thumping the rib cage, listening with his stethoscope. "I find it hard to believe you didn't notice your father's condition. Does he live with you?"

"He's not my father."

"The nurses said—"

"He's a priest."

The doctor considered this.

"Somebody should have noticed," he said. "Do you people even look at this man when he, whatever you call it, performs the service? I haven't seen anything like it since I worked at a refugee camp in Ethiopia." Corcoran glanced at Cody blankly. The doctor added, "Malnutrition. Your priest is starving to death."

There were complications—kidneys, heart, a case of bronchitis that was threatening to expand into pneumonia—and Lafon remained in the hospital, drifting in and out of consciousness, while Corcoran and Cody sat with him. The coach described the games the old man had missed. Cody found a *Cosmopolitan* in the lobby and thumbed through it. Corcoran nearly asked, "Can't you find something other than that garbage?" but he bit his tongue. As if reading his mind, Cody tossed the magazine in the trash. Corcoran kicked the boy, lightly, and Cody smiled and shrugged.

Finally a nurse entered and announced that several parishioners had been waiting for some time. Could the Corcorans please wrap up their visit? So the coach leaned close to the unshaven cheek and hairy ear and told Lafon they must leave. Did he want to pray or something before they went? The priest nodded, eyes closed. What now? Corcoran looked at Cody in desperation. The boy began reciting the Lord's Prayer.

The Corcorans had never been a religious family, but Cody kept the prayer plodding along, and the coach kept up most of the way, until the line about on earth as it is in heaven. But then the priest's eyes opened, glassy and tormented, as if glimpsing a terrible chimera. Corcoran said, "Forgive us this day our daily bread—" and then stumbled. He let Cody finish; he could not find his way to the end.

HELP

Dear Friend,

I am Mrs. Mariam Sese Seko, widow of late President Mobutu Sese Seko of Zaire, now known as Democratic Republic of Congo (DRC). I am moved to write you this letter in confidence—. Most of my husband's million[s] of dollars [were] deposited in Swiss bank[s] and other countries [and] coded for safe purpose because the new head of state, (Dr.) Mr. Laurent Kabila, has made arrangement[s] with the Swiss government and other European countries to freeze all my late husband's treasures—

I have deposited the sum [of] thirty million United State[s] dollars (U.S.$30,000,000.00) with a security company, for safekeeping. What I want you to do is to indicate your interest that you will assist us by receiving the money on our behalf.

—Recently received Hotmail message

My friends can't believe it. All they ever get is junk e-mail—baldness cures, coupons from Internet casinos, scams from online stockbrokers. They say, "How come nobody ever wants my help? I'd do it. I could receive the thirty million." I say, "Look, don't take it personally." The thing is, people trust me. They know that for me, it's not about the money. I just feel good about myself whenever I help a widow get her hands on the nest egg her late husband squirreled away, when a smile crinkles the face of an elderly generalissimo who learns that his life's savings have been converted to bullion that is stashed where class-action lawsuits won't ever find it.

Besides, it's not as easy as you might think. Everyone falls silent and glowers when you show up at some château in Martinique or pink-marble palace in Casablanca: the sullen playboy sons in maroon blazers, the balding former *chefs de gouvernement* in dark glasses, the tough guys in Armani suits with Glocks bulging in their shoulder holsters. Arguments break out about the wisdom of entrusting millions to an American drifter who shaves three times a week, wears shorts and a San Jose Sharks T-shirt to work, and has lost track of his own checking account. Things can turn ugly: broken chandeliers, bullet chips in the travertine walls, bodies that have to be fished out of the caviar tub and dumped in a shantytown in the middle of the night.

The only thing to do is to be as straightforward as possible. I say, "Folks, I sense some tension here today. The last thing I want is to cause hard feelings in the family. I can walk out right now and forget you ever e-mailed me."

That usually breaks the ice. Despite what you may have heard, Mrs. Mariam Sese Seko is an elegant lady who fluently speaks the French of her Brussels convent-school days. She asks, "What kind of cut are you talking about?"

A stocky man in a black suit explodes: "But you can't seriously—"

"Nguanda, shut up," she says. Then she turns to me. "Besides, you've done this sort of thing before, no? Ceauşescu's kids, the Duvaliers, Pol Pot?"

"Forgive me, Madam First Lady, but even if I had helped these people, I couldn't discuss it. But rest assured, I've got experience. And I usually get thirty percent."

You have to be discreet, but I can say this: I get around. Many's the time I fronted multimillion-dollar wire transfers for relatives of a late Persian Gulf head of state. I once flew to Hawaii to receive a container full of shoes for a gentle, modest lady who really doesn't deserve the ridicule she's suffered at the hands of the media. And people never stop and wonder how a former East African president who fled his nation penniless back in the late seventies came up with the cash for the home in Jidda, the Olympic-size pool, the powder-blue Camaro and turquoise Maserati, the gold-plated accordion he likes to finger while watching "Charlie's Angels" reruns.

Idi didn't trust me either, in the beginning, but nowadays he's e-mailing jokes and photos of his grandkids. Whenever I'm in town, we'll spend the evening eating sloppy joes, swigging from a bottle of twelve-year-old Glenfiddich, and watching "Nick at Nite." He has changed, you know. The old swagger is gone. He no longer wears the uniform and ivory-handled six-shooters, and he has bloated to Falstaffian proportions; he lumbers around in his skivvies and Muslim skullcap and cowboy boots. What would he do without me? To be honest, I feel a little sorry for him.

After a few hits of the hooch, Idi will strike up a tune on the accordion, and we sing:

She was a slender refugee, the apple of my eye.
She baked me a mighty tasty crocodile pie.
Singin', "Baby, I'm a-love you, till the day you die."

The man can get a little crazy when he drinks. Abruptly he'll grab his Kalashnikov, blow away the Chihuly glass on the mantelpiece, riddle the Peter Howson painting of Britney Spears. It's better to ignore this. Once one of his wives—Avin, the Algerian—came down to shush him, and he shot her, too.

Well, if I hadn't been there, who would have reached the crown prince on his mobile in Crawford, slipped those hundreds to the cops, found an Army-Navy store that would deliver a body bag at one in the morning in Jidda? Who would have helped Idi stumble off to bed as a fit of drunken remorse overcame him, or sat with him till his sobbing subsided and a steely and constricted look took hold on his face? Who would have comforted him when he said, "Sometimes I wonder if I'm going to Hell"?

"You, Idi? You're killing me, man. Come on. It's been a bad day, is all."

"I always end up shooting everybody: servants, wives, the kids."

"Hey, everyone loses his temper sometimes."

His bloodshot eyes settled on me. "I don't think I'll be needing your help in the future."

Right. That's what they always say. But soon he'll be running after me, he and everybody else. I'll log on to Hotmail and find—amid all those e-mails reading "New Pill Increases Penis by 26%" and "Law Degree Only $49.95"—a message from Madam First Lady or Baby Doc or Idi himself, pleading, "I need you now." I'll pack a bag, and I'm off for Zurich or the Cayman Islands. It's not that I think I'm special—anybody would do the same thing. You do it because you care.

DEAR LEADER

LET US CALL HER EUN-JU, FOR PEOPLE MAY DIE IF HER REAL NAME is revealed. Her own life is in danger, and her two sisters, her brother-in-law, and one surviving nephew remain at large south of the Tumen River, near the port of Hongwan, a city of apartment blocks without toilets, empty wharves populated by slump-shouldered cranes and rusty destroyers, a train station where the homeless sleep on the waitingroom seats or on the floor with the mice, and bony children who lie down in the alleys because after a certain point—thirty, thirty-five days, perhaps—they cannot stand any longer. The point is, it is illegal to flee the Democratic People's Republic of Korea, and the crime is compounded for party members (and Eun-ju is a member of this caste: a journalist). The security organs would arrest her relatives if they figured out the identity of this twenty-four-year-old woman, and there is not enough food to squander on prisoners in North Korea. The only ones definitely beyond the reach of the secret police are her mother and two infant nieces, all of whom died of pneumonia; Father, the person responsible for what happened, by now surely has also died: when Eun-ju fled to China, he was groaning from an advanced case of intestinal cancer, a fitting way to die in a famine, he said, and perhaps he has been buried, in her absence, in the cemetery overlooking the flood plains. Yet if anyone was culpable, it was he, for he urged her to flee, saying, "Go, you are young, you are beautiful" (though this could not possibly be true; she was balding at the time she left: strands of her hair clung to her fingers whenever she smoothed it). "At least one of the family should live. And some young Korean farmer in China will pay good money for you."

Let him be called Yong-shik. He is thirty-five years old, a sixth-grade graduate, a tiller of four-tenths of a hectare of soybeans and vegetables in China's Yanbian Korean Autonomous Prefecture. Yong-shik has never married, but his position is commonplace in rural Yanbian; the region is in crisis, its villages populated by Korean bachelor farmers. Innumerable girls were abandoned at birth and died in orphanages. The living disappeared at adulthood into the cities to work as prostitutes or serve Laochaoyang vodka in the karaoke bars or even, in the case of a single outstanding student he had once known, to study at Yanbian University. None of them, not even the simplest, a retarded girl twelve years his junior, was willing to spend her remaining five decades or more with Yong-shik, leading an ox back and forth plowing a field. The retarded girl was now a masseuse. Her mother refused his proposal the last time she was in town. "She already earns four times what you do; why would she marry you?" the mother said. Truth be told, he was a little relieved. He was no academician, but he did not know if he could enjoy life with a simpleton. He needed someone to cook, someone to lie with, someone to tell of his happiness when the bean shoots come up overnight after a rain; speaking softly, for they would not want to wake their infant son—in his mind there was no doubt that she would bear him a son. That she, too, might wish to talk as well on occasion did not occur to him. He had so much to say, and often he went for two or three days without speaking to anyone but the peasant squatting two holes over in the brick latrine that was the only toilet for several dozen houses on this street.

"Give us the paper, would you?" Yong-shik would say.

The man would grunt and hand over a copy of the *Yanbian Daily*. "Don't use the soccer results."

"Of course not." Yong-shik tore off the page with the ads for China Mobile and a miracle hair-restoration ointment and returned the rest. "Thank you," he said.

"You're welcome."

This passed for conversation on most days during the five years it took for Yong-shik to save up enough money for a wife.

■ They met one afternoon in February, twenty-three days after she left North Korea. An ethnic Korean marriage broker named Bong-il drove her to her new home near Yanji, rasping dire warnings all the way in the back seat of his smoky Land Cruiser while his driver adjusted the music on the stereo. "If you run away, we will find you, understand? He is paying good money for you, and we are men of our word. We'll return you, and you'll discover what an angry husband can do to a girl. I know this one guy, he chained his wife to the bed and gouged her eyes out the third time she tried to run away. If we don't find you, the police will, and you know what that means: back to Korea. Stay put. Even if he beats you, you'll be fed, unlike in Hongwan, right? You will live. Seems like a fair bargain." He threw his cigarette butt out the window and asked, "Are you listening?" She was. "Good," he said, "because I'm not trying to scare you, I hope you're happy, I truly do, you're such a pretty girl, or you will be when you fatten up and your hair fills in. I can see such things when anyone else in my place would think you're a throwaway, that's why I'm so good at this business: I get off on the potential of beauty, the withered rosebush that can be coaxed back to flower. I'm just explaining the situation, that's all. Anyway, you should thank me: I got you someone who was a cut above all these peasants. A wily man, makes a little money selling his produce in the markets. Incidentally, it's his prerogative to resell you if he wishes. Maybe that isn't so bad. Think of it this way: if you don't get along, maybe you'll end up with someone more compatible."

As they rounded a bend just out of Yanji, an enormous house came into view, standing on a bluff over the road and surrounded by a brick wall frosted along the top with the distant gleam of glass shards, and for a moment her heart leapt with the thought that she might be heading for a life of luxury on such an estate. But then Bong-il noticed her gaze and said, "Do you like that place? It's mine. She scoffs. I'm not kidding. There's a lot of money in girls. And, of course, I have other business ventures. You had no idea you were in the presence of such an important man, huh, little girl?"

There was a long silence as the Land Cruiser continued on to Yong-shik's village, then barreled past row upon row of attached brick houses—slum dwellings, really: single-story, each no larger than a villager's hut, and topped by swayback tile roofs and a clutter of crooked brick chimneys leaking coal smoke into a contused, yellow sky. The rows of homes were separated by dirt roads where children played hopscotch, cautiously, finding the rough spots, because yesterday a cold rain had washed away the snow and now everything was frozen mud. Several children stopped to watch the strange vehicle. It passed three white doors and a red one, each decorated with strips of red paper whose gold characters wished health and prosperity to all who entered; then finally it stopped, Bong-il leaning across Eun-ju to let her out. Or to hold her in, rather, because he pinned her in place and slipped a business card into her hand.

"If he decides to sell you, have him call me," Bong-il said. "Maybe I can broker someone better, once you fill out a little."

She got out and slammed the car door.

When Bong-il knocked, a farmer with a sun-creased face opened the door: a handsome jaw, intelligent eyes, a tiny wart by his nose, a super-abundance of moles. Yong-shik's overlarge paws were black with dirt, but he nonetheless shook Bong-il's soft, dank hand (Bong-il wiped his hand afterward with an embroidered handkerchief; Yong-shik dried his palm on his pants) and invited them through a concrete-floored entry filled with rakes, shovels, buckets, dried ears of corn hanging from the walls, a plow without a blade. Glancing frequently with mute wonder at Eun-ju, the farmer led them into the living quarters, a single room with a cooker built into the floor—a wood-fired unit covered by a lid the size of a truck's hubcap. A faucet poked its snout from the kitchen wall, but there was no sink, and a plastic trash barrel had been placed underneath it to catch the water. Everywhere there were signs that this was not North Korea: a twenty-kilo bag of rice sat in the corner, color calendars with pictures of girls in swimsuits hung on the walls, and there was electricity to squander: a miniature black-and-white television buzzed with a broadcast of a soccer game. Astoundingly, a bird cheeped from within Yong-shik's shirt pocket. He patted himself down and removed a black object the size of a wallet, which he opened and spoke into. "She just got here," he said. "I'll call back." A phone without a cord. He folded and pocketed it. Blushing, he explained, "My mother." Then he remembered his manners and asked everyone to sit on the floor.

Yong-shik surveyed the woman, a scrawny refugee with cherry-red lipstick supplied by Bong-il, dressed in a fake Adidas warm-up suit, recently purchased, over which she wore her only remaining article of clothing from North Korea: a padded overcoat with a chevron pattern woven into the fabric.

"Why is her hair so short?" he asked.

The broker waved away his concern. "Hunger. You should have seen it when she got here: as thin as an old woman's. They're often like that when they leave. Anyway, you can see it's already growing back, glossy and thick. We've been fattening her up for you."

Yong-shik stared at Eun-ju and opened his mouth as if wishing to say something, but he was struck dumb. He turned to Bong-il for help.

"Her personality—how is it?"

"Quiet. Very kind. Obedient."

"And she is capable of bearing children?"

"Absolutely. She was inspected by a doctor, a woman doctor."

This was entirely untrue, but it mollified Yong-shik, for he said, "I think we agreed upon twenty-five hundred yuan?"

"This one is three thousand."

"You can't do that; you already said—"

"There were extra payments to the border guards on both sides, more than I expected. This is a dangerous business, and I risked my life to bring you your heart's desire. Besides, look at her, she's worth it: a lovely girl, the future mother of your sons. There's this rich guy in Yanji wanted her for a karaoke club, said he would pay double whatever you offered, but I said a girl like this should go to a decent man. What's five hundred? If you don't like her, you can always make a profit on the resale."

Yong-shik glowered at the broker, then at Eun-ju, as if she were somehow complicit in this. She gave a sad, helpless shrug, and his expression softened into a look of shy inquiry, as if to ask, Well, then, do you think we can stand each other? Her eyebrows arched in reply: We shall see. This made him smile, and he nodded, almost bowed, a motion of the shoulders rather than his head, and began counting out the money from a candy box that he kept in the wardrobe. Bong-il's hitherto dour face split in a broad grin. Three thousand yuan was everything this farmer possessed, it was obvious, and it flattered the broker's vanity, as it might flatter a heroin dealer's, to offer a commodity so achingly desired by the buyer.

Yong-shik handed over the money without meeting Bong-il's gaze, full of glad bonhomie, then endured the broker's congratulations, his slaps on the back, his assurances that he would not regret this. For that matter, Bong-il nearly blurted out, Not to worry, she was terrific in bed, never mind that the age, twenty-whatever, was a little old for his tastes; he preferred to sample the thirteen-, fourteen-year-olds that the pimps and millionaires purchased—or at least his face said all that as he gave one last happy wink at Eun-ju. Then, seeing he was unwanted, he bounced out, whistling as he strode to the car, where the driver slumped, head flung back and mouth open, as if murdered at the wheel, but he quickened when his boss rapped on the glass. Yong-shik shut the door and returned to this new presence in his household: a wife.

For a moment the two sat together. He reached for her hand, calculated at what point he might properly propose they go to bed, then blushed as she read his thoughts. Instead, he said, "I understand you were a reporter."

"Yes, but it means nothing. I wrote what they told me."

"You have an education?"

"I graduated from Kim Il-Sung University, in Pyongyang."

"I used to long to go to the university. I excelled in math. But I dropped out of school to help my father on the farm, so I'm an uneducated man. I hope you won't find me too dull." A self-mocking grin tugged at his mouth as he said this, and she could not help smiling.

"I am sure farming is an interesting occupation, as well."

"You're the first woman I have ever met who thought so." They contemplated this. Momentarily it occurred to him to suggest, "Would you like some tea?"

"Please."

"There's a box on the shelf there. I'd like a cup, too. And as you see, the kettle stands beside it."

■ Yong-shik was an innocent, just as Eun-ju had been when she left Hongwan, and their first attempts were abruptly concluded by his premature enthusiasm, a phenomenon that she in all honesty hoped would continue, but by the third night they had succeeded, or so he thought, for afterward his heart was enraptured and melancholy at once, and he kissed her face and shoulders again and again, then spoke of the son he wanted, of the joy of family, of the way his mother and his father used to stealthily rustle about at night under the covers when they thought he was asleep, and for a long time, until he was seven or eight years old, he thought they were looking for something they had lost; he almost volunteered to help, but something, even in childhood, had held him back. But after he nodded off, Eun-ju lay awake trembling, averting her interior gaze from the sunspot on her heart, grasping instead at random distractions as they fluttered like moths through her mind: Father, his strong hands, the sadness that settled upon him when I came home from school and recited my lessons: *Our National Father, who shines upon us like the sun,* and after mumbling, "He would be proud of you, daughter," he sat with a newspaper in his lap, not reading, but staring at the wall, unable to be drawn from his catatonic melancholy. No, something happier: think of Mother, long ago, when there was food, returning from a trip to Vladivostok with a bag of chocolates wrapped in shiny pictures of camels and palm trees, which she placed on a shelf out of reach as I stamped and said, "I want I want I want," an insufferable brat; think of home, of the candlelight glittering on the frost patches the size of mattresses growing on the walls; think of work, of the spaghetti of electrical wiring stapled along the ceiling of the newsroom, of the baby cockroaches that infested the desk drawers, of the broken Soviet refrigerator in the stinking canteen without food, of the hours of sitting through speeches and parades in order to write something that meant nothing to no one at anytime ever:

> Some 1,500 white herons have been visiting Mangyongdae, the time-honored holy land of revolution, every day. The birds fly in flocks above President Kim Il-sung's native home, stay in forests on Mangyong Hill overnight and fly to the house at dawn. They sit on willow trees on the pond near the house before flying toward the River Taedong. This phenomenon occurs every day, according to officials of the Mangyongdae Revolutionary Museum. This wonderful scene has been witnessed every year since this time three years ago after the death of the President. The pine trees covered with white herons in summer remind one of a beautiful scene in winter in a fable. Witnesses said the new sight of Mangyongdae shows that even the birds miss the president, who descended from heaven.

(But even as you wrote—mindlessly, the Hangul letters goose-stepping from the fog of the unconscious—you thought, So he was anointed by birds? Meaning, they're to blame for all this? You tensed from repressed hysterical laughter, faked a sneeze, tried to stop thinking, So could we alter the historical dialectic if we left out some poisoned bird seed? Except that there's no seed to be had north of the DMZ, all of it having been consumed, along with the cattle feed and rice.) As she lay there beside Yong-shik, however, the dark interior tide would not be stayed by distractions, and she gave herself over to the flood of hot panic, remembering the night Bong-il unlocked the shed and called her, rather than the two teenage girls she had heard whimpering every night from the main house, remembering the vodka smell of his sweat and his fatness atop her and the pain of his rubbery thrusting as she turned her head to the side and bit her knuckles. Lying here with Yong-shik, she cried, but silently, because she did not wish to awaken her husband.

Dear Jesus, let me find peace here. Dear Buddha, do not let them arrest me. Dear Leader, it is treason, but I do not want to die in your brilliant present reality.

Shifting in the dark, Eun-ju held Yong-shik because she had no one else.

■ It was obvious that this farmer was crazy about her. When the pussy willows budded in March, he brought home a bouquet and put them in a bottle for her. He took down his girlie calendars after she made a face at them. He inquired about her likes and dislikes with the frown of a schoolboy seeking through diligence to make up for a long absence from class. This is not to say he did not have expectations of her—cooking, cleaning, scrubbing his farm clothes in a plastic washbasin—and he did his best to issue his orders sternly, as was expected of a husband. Yet, however severe he attempted to sound, he always smiled, and his face quickly assumed the smitten puppy-dog expression he wore in her presence. Nevertheless, she soon learned that in China, too, there were ideological demands: he was stunned to discover that she did not follow any soccer team, and informed her that she must now root for Aodong; it would cause disharmony in the household if they were not in accord on this matter. "Aodong it will be," Eun-ju said. He nodded, but the look of suspicion in his eyes was entirely familiar: he was uncertain of her orthodoxy. Yet Yong-shik respected her enough to ask what her favorite book was so he could read it; he was in awe of her education.

At first she thought it was a trap—she did not yet trust him—and she said that she had always found Chairman Mao's sayings deeply influential. But seeing the look on his face, she confessed that she did not especially like books. One always believed that the written word could be full of joy and love and death and betrayal, but all you read at home were classics such as *Kim Jong-il in His Younger Days* and *U.S. Troops' Bestial Tyranny Flayed,* and despite the longing you felt while gazing with your eyes unfocused at the pages of any given tome, imagining that words could arrange themselves into a living force, one could not bring life to the stories about female guerrillas tearing off pieces of their tunics to create a quilt for the infant Kim as Japanese bullets whistled past, not to mention entire libraries full of industrial production statistics and *juche* theory. She cut herself short, abruptly stayed by a different worry: that she had spoken over his head; at all costs she did not want to insult his intellectual pride, lest he announce that he had had enough of this headstrong woman and get rid of her.

But he nodded gravely and said, "I get the same feeling reading the agricultural news in the papers here. There's so much they could say—exposés of party leaders who manipulate the rice cooperative, stories about how the hog farm is polluting the river—but it's all harvest reports and five-year plans, even in the middle of a drought."

As the weeks passed, Eun-ju's fears that Yong-shik would sell her diminished. But although she had, on her first day in China, removed from her lapel the medal of the deceased yet ever-living head of state and Great Leader, President Kim Il-sung, grinning (the frowning medal had been replaced some time ago), and pinned it inside her coat pocket where she would not lose it, she dared not throw it away; for if the unthinkable happened and she were picked up by the Chinese police and sent home, she did not want to arrive at the frontier without her medal, as its presence might mitigate her treason: I never lost my faith, I never ceased to long for the fulfillment of human evolution achieved in the Great Leader and his son, the Dear Leader, Kim Jong-il. She never went outdoors unless absolutely necessary, and shopping in the open market was her greatest anxiety: elbowing through the crowds in broad daylight, ordering eels and bok choy, scooping paprika from the basket at a spice seller's stall, always glancing around to make sure the people pressing close were grannies with shopping bags and not young men in leather and sunglasses ready to grab her, for her fear was not only of police but also of other brokers, who had been known to kidnap North Korean girls already here in China and deliver them to other buyers. For the first few weeks, she drank almost no tea and consumed as little water as possible so that she would limit her trips to the community latrine, though eventually she came to see that the neighbor women, all ethnic Koreans, regarded her sympathetically, and two of them dropped by one day to offer tips on how to dress and wear her makeup like a Chinese.

Often at night, however, after descending through a tunnel of relentless dark, she found herself once again lying beside Bong-il as he snored, and she thought, There's a knife in the kitchen and no one to stop me, I could find it and plunge it into his neck. With her heart pounding, she crept to the kitchen and felt about in the shadows, always unable to find the knife, and then as her eyes adjusted she made out a dark spot in the wall. A set of yellowed human teeth was nibbling a hole from the other side, the cuspids recessed like Bong-il's. She woke herself; and, rolling over in the moonlight, she looked at her husband, his mouth gaping innocently, a yawning infant. Hush, she thought, hush, as though it were he who had awakened terrified. She dared not turn on the light, for fear of either waking Yong-shik or catching the attention of a police patrol who would then drop by to investigate. She did not know if they would do this here in China, but old precautions were hard to get rid of. She found a bottle of beer and drank it in the dark.

When May Day came, there was no avoiding one task out-of-doors. Yong-shik insisted that she help with the plowing. At first it frightened her, working in the bright fields in plain view of the cars, trucks, cyclists, and red taxicabs that crept along the muddy road toward Yanji. Eun-ju led an ox team back and forth as Yong-shik followed, steering the plow and exhorting the beasts, "Come on! Get! Yah!" Sinking ankle deep in the soil, she trudged along, stone-footed, the clay clinging to her boots, but despite her anxiety, she began to enjoy herself, so long had it been since she worked outside and felt the sun warming her skin. The last time she had trudged across a rural field was when General Secretary Kim himself had overseen the land realignment project in North Phyongan Province, and she had covered his speech. Dear Leader: she was surprised to discover that this hero commander-in-chief, inventor of nuclear physics, astrophysicist, greatest golfer known to man, and immortal botanist and biologist who had once, at four years of age, discovered why chickens raise their beaks when they drink and why there are no black flowers—that this poet and genius was a fat little man in a Mao suit with bouffant hair and yellow teeth, lecturing everyone on Marxist doctrine as it relates to land reclamation, cracking jokes with his generals and regional party apparatchiks about the girls they had found him from the cooperative farms in Jongju city and Uiju and Kwaksan provinces. And a blasphemous thought wormed its way into her mind: that he was merely stupid, this Son of the Most High who strode around waving his pointer, who with his Father in Heaven had sown the seeds of everlasting joy and prosperity across the land. Yet she suppressed this thought and sang his praises in the story she filed. She could do it drunk or asleep, so familiar was the speech she was given to paraphrase:

> Feasting his eyes on the large standardized fields, he noted with great satisfaction that provincial party members and other working people, People's Army soldiers, shock brigade members from other provinces, and engineers involved in the Land Realignment Campaign have completely changed the appearance of the countryside by creditably finishing the difficult and gigantic project on a high qualitative level. He lavished praise on their great achievements and thanked them. He noted that all the soldiers and people involved in the large-scale nature-transforming project have carried out their enormous assignments in a matter of several months in the indomitable revolutionary spirit of soldiers who were pressed for everything, though the people's enemies had said that even a few years would not be enough to complete the task. He added that this is a world-startling miracle that has forced the craven American aggressor to go down on his knees in awe of the achievements of the Korean people.
>
> He pointed out that the present brilliant reality in North Phyongan Province clearly shows how powerful is the might of our army and people who are rushing ahead in a high-pitched spirit with an iron faith that once they are determined, they can do anything. He said that realignment must be done throughout the whole land so that none of its former contours could be recognized, and likewise the kulaks and hirelings of the imperialists must be crushed in their attempts to secretly and illegally hoard food crops for personal benefit.

"Ha!" Yong-shik called behind the oxen. "Ha! Get up!"

As she led the snorting, muddy beasts back and forth, Eun-ju gazed across the crests and valleys of Yanbian, and from here she could see half a dozen other ox teams, the men always slogging along behind the plow, the women (for those farmers lucky enough to be married) always leading the oxen.

It is right that I will end my days as a farmwife. Working the soil will be a penitence for every word I have written.

"You're drifting left," Yong-shik called, and she yanked on the reins and pulled the oxen in line.

━ The wedding was put off till the planting was done in May, and by that time she had missed a period and was suffering from alternating bouts of terrific hunger and nausea that caused her to bolt for the yard and throw up. She told Yong-shik she was not yet used to rich food, for she did not want to raise his expectations just yet, and she was afraid the family would insist that she have an abortion if this child's sex proved to be incorrect, for she wanted to protect this being inside her, the prawn-like form, the tiny appendages that would become legs and arms. (And the child likewise would not survive if she were repatriated to a North Korean labor camp. In Yanbian it was said that the Dear Leader kept the national bloodline pure by letting babies conceived in China die of exposure upon birth, or having them dispatched with a forceps pushed into the soft top of the skull.) So she kept the news secret, telling herself she would wait another month or two. Yet even without suspecting her condition, the family saw her as a treasure, an enhancement of their status—My son, you know, has found himself a wife—and she clung to this observation as evidence that the time had passed in which it was possible to resell her.

In June they rented a maroon bridal gown at great expense and held a private ceremony. There was no way they could register the marriage, for she was an illegal, and this meant that her son or daughter (please make it a boy!) would not be able to attend school, enter university, drive a car, or find a job; but that was years away, and she could hope things would change by then. She received a great number of gifts: a wardrobe, a new dress, a set of plates, a cutting board and several knives, clothes from a cousin who worked in the market. The women prepared a feast such as Eun-ju had never seen in her life: many varieties of kimchi, rice and beans, fern salads, minute salted fish, and beef *bulgogi*. The only time she had ever heard of such a feast in North Korea was at the April Eighth Cooking Festival at the Pyongyang Noodle House, a festival open only to the senior party leaders. (She had not been allowed to attend the event she was covering, yet she could smell the food, taste it, as she wrote, hungry.)

Even then, she had heard nothing about the delicacy that was served at her wedding, a "shit dog"—dogs raised in cages where they consumed their own feces. The slaughter took place in public, in the alley behind Yong-shik's cousin's apartment. Looping a noose around the neck of the dog, Yong-shik's father, Yun-jong, hoisted it by the throat while Yong-shik beat it to death with a stool, and the provisional contentment that Eun-ju had attained (I am alive, I eat every day, I care for this Yong-shik and he is a decent man) crumbled within. Yun-jong set to butchering the dog with quick slices of the knife, skinning the fur off the tallowy ribcage, and Yong-shik gave his bride a proud glance, knowing that dog would have been beyond the means of any but the richest in North Korea, strays long ago having been eaten. But only when he wiped the sweat from his sockets (first the right shoulder, then the left) did he see his wife's face as she fled indoors.

He followed her upstairs, through the apartment, and out onto the balcony, where he comforted her while trying not to attract any more attention than a groom normally draws while whispering to his bride in view of everyone with his face spattered in dog's blood.

"What's the matter?"

"It's nothing. It will pass." Eun-ju smiled. If the Democratic People's Republic teaches one anything, it is to perfect a public face of joy and optimism, whatever fires burn within.

"You're upset about the dog."

"I've just never seen that before."

"You are too innocent for a farmwife. That's your problem." The thought pleased Yong-shik, and before returning to his task he squeezed her hand. He left blood on it.

The panic slowly subsided, and she calmed herself thinking of Yong-shik.

He is a good man, he is, he is. You cannot ask for more than decency and a rugged handsomeness, too, especially when you consider what might have awaited you here. And the capacity of his mind is surprising for an unlettered man. I can be happy with him. Maybe I already am. Maybe this is all happiness is. Not being hungry. Not being beaten. Not lying.

■ He drank too much that day, and they barely made it home on his motorbike, wobbling around the corners, laughing, sounding his horn as they zipped past a car that had broken down by the road. But that night it was Yong-shik's turn for insomnia. He started awake as a lightning storm marched in, and he could not believe his foolhardiness, driving drunk, blaring his way through town. Eun-ju moaned in her sleep. Gently he took her hand. He was not blind to the sadness that lay upon her like a heavy cloak, and it dawned on him that he had purchased a bottomless reservoir of pain along with a bride. Rain pelted the windows, and the lightning flashed, defining her face in a blue relief. Moments later (*two, three, four*) thunder rattled the windows. Yong-shik was desperately afraid of losing her.

Eventually she rolled over and issued a little gasp. She was crying.

He asked, "What's the matter, honey?"

"Nothing."

"Was the wedding a disappointment?"

"No, it was wonderful."

"Honey, I am sorry the dog upset you."

"The dog doesn't matter. It just reminded me of something."

"Of what?"

For a long time, Eun-ju did not answer. Just as he concluded that she had fallen asleep, her voice came from the electrostatic dark. "There was this boy who somehow stole a cake from Kang, a local party leader who had gotten rich reselling the rice donated by the imperialist aggressors—he was selling a kilo for one-hundred fifty won: two months' wages. I don't know how it happened, whether the boy broke into Kang's apartment or stole it from his car or what, but he came running down the street, saw it was a dead end, and panicked and banged through the door of this state store—you see such places in Korea, the shelves bare nowadays save for candles, matchsticks, maybe a bottle of vegetable oil, some Victorious Vodka. It was a fearful sight—this little stick figure crouching between the radiator and a bench, choking down frosting like a wild animal. Then, Kang came puffing in. 'Spit it out, you little traitor,' he said. The boy swallowed. Kang seized up the bench and hit him again and again, staved the boy's skull in. He left the body there in a pool of violet for the shopkeeper to dispose of. This was not hard to do. This was at the height of the famine. There were corpse trucks."

"You saw all this?"

He felt a movement: a nod.

"You get so you don't feel," Eun-ju said. "I hadn't thought of it in a long time. So many things happen. Everyone's hungry."

He had always avoided asking how she had gotten to China, fearing that it would include details that he could not bear to hear. But now he inquired, "Surely it was no easy thing to flee the country?"

"My father had connections; he was the one who sold me."

Yong-shik sat up, hugging his knees.

"I agreed," she said. "There was no other way. I could have died there, and the family was desperate. I told you my father has cancer."

He nodded with his chin on his knees.

"Father was a ranking railroad official—so was my mother before she passed away, for that matter; she had been to Russia several times to work with her counterparts in Khasan and Vladivostok. But because of his illness, Father hasn't worked since before the time the People's Supreme Court hanged the Seven Lackeys of the Imperialists and their Southern Stooges in Kim Il-sung Stadium. Perhaps you heard that here. No? They said the world media were following it. As it happened, Father had worked closely with two of the traitors before their execution. There was a time when we lived in terror that he would be arrested, too. Perhaps with Father's illness, he was out of the way and the security organs decided it wasn't worth pursuing him. I'm speculating. In any case, things became very hard for us after that. Mother had already passed away by then. At my work there were struggle sessions. We felt something was coming, that I would soon be arrested. But Father knows certain wealthy men of influence, military officers, party members who were active disassembling factories and selling lathes and machine tools to China as scrap. He is very sick, and he spends his days lying in our two-room apartment, wan and skeletal. I used to sit with him massaging his limbs where they hurt. The blackouts last eighteen, twenty hours a day in the residential districts, and the central heating has hardly worked since I was a girl, so he lies there in his outdoor coat, heaped with blankets, his mouth fixed in an expression of rage and bewilderment. He is a very good man, a brave man, and now he is in pain all the time—never sleeps more than forty-five minutes at a time. Slept. Sometimes I'm afraid he has passed away by now."

There was another long pause in her story, and when a flash illuminated a glittering trail on her cheek, Yong-shik wiped it away.

"The apartment always smelled of illness, of medicine, of ginseng snake wine, burning ginger, moxibuxion cotton. But in the end there was no money for food or medicine. We talked many times about what our options were, and I agreed with my father that finding a husband in China was the best one. Still, it was a shock to come home from work one Friday and find a man squatting there in a Chinese suit and white socks and a watch that hung loose on his wrist. His face shone with health—the fat cheeks and pellucid eyes of one who has never starved. 'Last time I saw you, you were just a little girl, and look at you now,' he said. It was Kang. Obviously he did not remember or notice that I had been there when he killed the boy. I glanced at Father in alarm, but he wouldn't meet my eye.

"Kang scrutinized me. Astonishingly, he began prodding my ribs. 'She's thin,' he said.

"Father said, 'We eat simply; she is a good cook in these hard times and can produce a delicious dinner from a little shredded bark and grass mixed with maybe a couple tablespoons of rice when it's available. I do not complain; as the Dear Leader says, we must toughen ourselves in the battle against the American aggressor. But she will fatten up when she gets real food again.'

"'The question is, is she healthy? No diseases? I see you are a sick man yourself, Comrade Lee.'

"'Oh, she's very healthy,' Father said. He gave me this despairing glance. 'She has always been a good girl and a party member. No boyfriends, nothing serious.'

"'How old is she?' Kang asked.

"'Twenty-two,' I said.

"He glanced at me. 'She seems older.'

"'She's hungry. Everybody is.'

"'We will say twenty-two. She's a beautiful girl, no obvious blemishes. Yes, I think we can find her a husband. If only she were fourteen or fifteen, we might find her a wealthy man indeed. As it is, I can give you seven hundred fifty won or five kilos of rice. Your choice.'

"Father chose the rice. The family was hungry and he could also barter it. I had a half hour to pack a few things. We left for the border that night."

Yong-shik lay back down. The thunderstorm was tramping away, its flashes distant, the thunderclaps insufficient to rattle the windows, a faint rumble now.

"Are you angry with me," he asked, "for buying you?"

Yes, I am, she wanted to say. I am not a piece of furniture, a bicycle, a cake. I am angriest of all because I am unable to hate you, because I might even love you, because I'm afraid I would love any man who provided for me and showed a little gentleness after such deprivation. However, she only said, "How can I be angry? Without you I'd be dead."

"It's not the way I would have chosen to find you, but it turned out right in the end, eh? I thought I would live my whole life alone, that I would never find a wife. And then I was so afraid that I'd spend all this money and we'd hate each other. I know it was hard for you, but you did your duty, helping your family. And if we make some money off this crop, we can get a little cash to your family. Everything will work out. We can get treatment for your father. Maybe we can bring him here. Do you think they'd allow that?"

Yong-shik slipped his hand inside the blouse of her pajamas and stroked her abdomen. Did he suspect that she was pregnant? No, he was tracing a line from her navel down to the thicket, slipping two fingers inside.

She rolled toward him, grasped him gently, began a motion of the wrist, up and down. She said, "You won't ever sell me, will you, honey?"

Stunned, he pinned her shoulders to the mattress. "How can you ask that after today? My entire family—"

"Because Bong-il told me—"

"Hush." Then humbly, as if fearing where such a declaration might lead, Yong-shik said to a woman for the first time in his adult life, "I love you."

As her husband unbuttoned her blouse, Eun-ju said, "You know I love you."

Perhaps she meant it. In any case, what else could she say?

━ Two days later, Yong-shik set off at dawn, four o'clock in summer in this part of China, and by the time Eun-ju had left to go shopping, he was twenty kilometers away, slowly driving a heap of vegetables into town past a long line of peasants on their backwards tricycles while the trucks rattled by spilling gravel. As she walked home with a duffel bag full of groceries, she was preoccupied with thoughts of her family in Hongwan. She recalled a memory from nearly two decades ago, her father saying, "Up!" and throwing her almost into the blurry canopy of blossomy trees in Stalin Park, then she came rushing down toward his big eyes and open mouth, to be caught only at the last moment. "Again!" she cried. "Again, Daddy!" It was one of her earliest memories, but then as she tried to cling to it, strangely, it was as if she were stationary and Father were being cast away from her, and now, walking along a dirt road in Northeast China, she was seized by the conviction that he had died. He would be lying in his coffin—his blue pallid face, the mortification that ages the body when the spirit departs, so that within hours he would appear to be seventy and not fifty-two—and she heard the state burial liturgy, the name of the Father and the Son, the Great Leader and the Dear Leader, blessed duality, and heading down Central Street with a heavy duffel of food, she grieved at the ubiquity of mourning during a general famine that would have drowned out any sorrow over the death of one middle-aged cancer victim. She had just left the main road for the warren of alleyways in the neighborhood where she lived when someone grabbed her from behind.

"Get in," he said.

"Let me go!"

"Get in."

Bong-il. Shoving her toward the Land Cruiser. His driver, too, along with a powerful man who pinned her other arm behind her back.

"I'll scream. Help!"

"You want to scream?" Bong-il said. "You want the cops to come? Go ahead."

Eun-ju looked around on the street. A child was dribbling a soccer ball against a brick wall. He was watching her.

"So shut up and get in the car," said Bong-il.

Bong-il settled beside her while the bodyguard and the driver claimed the front seats, and he removed a handful of sunflower seeds from his pocket as the vehicle accelerated. The odors of sweat and after-shave filled the interior. He stuck a few seeds in his mouth and began cracking them, separating them with his tongue, plucking the husks from his lips to flick out the window.

"Want some?"

She ignored this. "What do you want with me?"

"Don't look so angry. It's good news. I came back to rescue you from a life of drudgery. I couldn't get you out of my mind, particularly after I saw you on your so-called wedding day. You didn't notice me? I thought you did, the way you started. I was driving by, and I caught a glimpse of this vision of beauty, in that maroon dress of yours, standing on the balcony, and I had my driver pull over. You can't imagine how stunned I was. Your hair's coming in fine, very pretty at that length, very modern. And I thought, I was right all along about that girl. I should have trusted my instincts and held onto you for a while longer. And then this fuckwit farmer comes out in his borrowed suit and starts tugging at your arm; and, if I may say so, it was obvious you were downright peeved at him. Poor girl. Life is a long, long time to spend with someone you dislike."

"I don't dislike him."

Bong-il laughed and popped another pinch of seeds in his mouth. "So anyway, I had an idea: a kidnapping. I'm taking you off the hands of this farmer, putting you in a place where you'll have a better life, maybe a little spending money for clothes and baubles if you're a good girl. I've got a better man for you."

"I don't want anyone else."

"Shut up. It's me. Do you understand? I already have a wife, but she's just a stupid little girl and she won't get in your way. You can imagine what it's like to be married to a teenager. Music, hair, parties. I told her we need another maid, but you don't need to take orders from her. Only from me. Who knows? Maybe if things turn out well, I'll sell her, and it will just be us, you and me."

"My husband is going to find me."

"Husband? Oh, you mean the guy who bought you for three thousand yuan? Fuck the stupid farmer. If I'm feeling generous and you don't irritate me too much, maybe I'll find him a replacement bride. What do you care? You saw where I live, a mansion. You'll stay there with me. Your new master. Ha ha, your Dear Leader."

The Land Cruiser was doing seventy kilometers an hour when Eun-ju stepped out. For a moment she was tumbling on the abrading gravel. Then a concrete pinnacle rose from the road and struck her head, and an inkwell exploded before her eyes.

■ On his first day back from his vacation, Inspector Yang with the Foreign Crimes Unit received an order to carry out his least favorite duty: returning a refugee. He found the woman in the dispensary cell, where the doctor, himself an ethnic Korean, at first argued that she could not possibly be handed over in this condition. But he was a state budget worker, and when his duty was made clear by the garrison commander, he signed her release papers. Yang escorted the prisoner, handcuffed and bandaged, to a taxicab outside, where the driver was instructed to head for the border. The two men passed the time chatting in Chinese, which the girl, it was obvious, did not understand. Inspector Yang was glad that the driver was a Han. They understood the necessity of this kind of work. "Those Koreans would overrun the whole region if you guys didn't stop them," the driver said. "There wouldn't be a single human being from the DMZ to the Tumen River. They'll all be here." Yang nodded, but it was an uncomfortable ride. He glanced at the prisoner, the black eyes, the bloodied ear, the arm in a sling. The girl was so frightened, it was as if she was in shock. All the way to the border, sixty kilometers, she stared ahead, saying nothing.

■ They stopped for a half hour to fill out a sheaf of papers at the border guard station on the Chinese side, then walked across the bridge to the halfway point, where the borderline was painted on the asphalt. It was summer now, and she was wearing no coat, and so she arrived without her medal of Kim Il-sung, an act of treason in itself. The North Korean border guard did not even wait until the prisoner was on his side of the line before smashing her in the eye with his fist.

"Did you like fucking those Chinese?" he said.

Eun-ju began weeping, gulping out sobs that had been building up for months, for years, for decades, for at that moment she was ancient, burdened by grief, by pain, by isolation, by men, by the prospect of giving birth in a labor camp to a baby who would be murdered as it drew its first breath, by the fear of dying alone in a very small place. It occurred to her now that she had never told Yong-shik she was pregnant.

Inspector Yang watched as the border guard dragged the girl to a building on the other bank and shoved her through the door. Sighing, he returned to his taxi. "Let's get out of here."

The driver had seen everything from the bank, and he remarked, "They're all shits, North Koreans."

The inspector bit his pen. Somehow it seemed disloyal to the fraternity of men in uniform to acknowledge this comment.

"Maybe she'll find her way back," the driver said. "I hear it happens. They bribe their way out."

Yang shrugged. "Somebody should do something," he said vaguely. "It always ends like this."

THE TIN MAN

FOR A WEEK BEFORE HE ATTENDED THE CONVENTION IN CHICAGO, Christian Sheehan lay awake at night imagining the great city of steel mills and Beaux-Arts skyscrapers and neighborhoods still inhabited by the ghosts of the St. Valentine's Day Massacre. He would be there for six days. Eleven years ago, before his senior year of college, he had passed through O'Hare on his way home to Spokane after visiting his girlfriend in Louisville, and the view out his airplane window, of the skyline along Lake Michigan, had not stirred any particular desire to tarry. He had always planned to become a young tycoon in a major city, maybe New York or even London or Rome, and there would be plenty of time to explore great metropolises on his own terms, not as a broke kid with a backpack who would have to find a park to sleep in.

But now he was a thirty-two-year-old actuary in the Spokane office of an insurance company whose clients were primarily wheat farmers, and he had rooted himself with seeming permanence in a city of two hundred thousand. Though he was single, he never dated. This left him plenty of time to play racquetball or hunt deer or sit in coffeehouses sipping espresso while thumbing through the *Journal of Business* ("serving Spokane and Kootenai counties"). Once, on a whim, he and a buddy hopped a freight train to Missoula. When they arrived they wandered the town for a few hours, split a pizza and a pitcher of beer, then caught the next train back to Spokane. Christian was sometimes invited for dinners or barbecues at the homes of married friends. Any single women who happened to be present would inevitably ignore him, while the wives were always especially attentive and kind. At the office he occasionally encountered clients who were missing a hand or an arm from combine accidents, and indeed one such man worked in Christian's department. These maimed individuals did not seem to mind Christian's face. Sometimes they asked him what had happened.

When he arrived at Midway that week, he caught a cab to the Loop and checked into a hotel with palatial staircases and a columned Second Empire-style lobby. His room looked out across an air shaft at another wing of the building, where a plump, blond Latina wearing a bra and nothing else could be seen cleaning her ear with the corner of a towel. Then she removed a pair of panties from her suitcase and stepped into them. The intimacy shocked him, and for an hour or so he was deeply in love with her. At home his apartment window looked out on ponderosa pines and a swift, glassy bend in the Spokane River upstream from the falls. The only people he saw on the banks were fishermen and middle-aged couples who brought their grandchildren to feed the ducks and geese. Thus the view from his hotel window seemed to indicate possibilities in this city. Love, for one.

Or so, Christian thought, run the fantasies of the self-deluded.

That week he ditched most of the sessions he had signed up for and instead explored the downtown. At first he simply wandered the Loop, buying a "Windy City" T-shirt at a pharmacy, stopping for coffee in a café, crossing repeatedly under the bolted superstructure of the El, where the trains roared along three stories above street level. From across Congress Parkway he surveyed Washington Library, like a Central Asian sandstone fortress that had been conquered in an imperial age and crowned with copper battlements and grotesque dragon gods. He circled past hotels and shoe outlets and a bakery exhaling its warm, doughy breath, then cut down a crowded street where a man wearing a tattered ID on a string around his neck was yelling, "*StreetWise!* One dollar!" For some reason he became offended when Christian gave him exactly one dollar for a copy. He followed Christian for a block, saying, "Come on, man, give me a blessing! I got kids. Give me another dollar. Look at y'all, big fat wallet, y'all-ass can afford an extra buck." Christian lost the man by the Daley Center amid swarms of lawyers in suits who were rushing, he imagined, to hearings involving crooked aldermen or the owners of Mob-connected trucking firms.

Each time he ventured out, his walks circled farther from his hotel. Strolling along the river on Upper Wacker Drive, he came to the Michigan Avenue drawbridge, where the foundations of Fort Dearborn were laid out in brass plaques on the sidewalk. North of the river the air smelled not of the steel mills or slaughterhouses he had expected, but of chocolate. Across from the neo-Gothic Tribune Tower a dark woman with beautiful lips and bloodshot eyes perched on a bronze sofa and told her woes to a sculpture of a television psychiatrist. At the Water Tower, with its stone facing like rumpled manila paper, five husky men wearing nametags from a prison guards' convention were studying a copy of the *Sun-Times*. One of them beckoned Christian and asked how to get to Chinatown.

"Sorry, no idea. I'm new here."

"You feeling all right, buddy?" the guard asked.

"Outstanding," Christian said, and for some reason they all laughed.

Otherwise, no one spoke to Christian as he walked. Nearly everyone in Chicago strode along without glancing right or left, and he took advantage of the anonymity to study the faces coming toward him, something he never did in Spokane, for people there always stared back in an instant of incomprehension, registered dismay, and then quickly looked away, as if by doing so they were granting him some small mercy. There was nothing wrong with the structure of Christian's face—lean, beak-nosed, round-jawed, possibly even handsome, he had once felt—but his skin had a ghastly stone pallor, grayest on the front-facing planes, less so on the sides, with flesh-colored question marks coiled within the ashen tones of his ears.

This was the result of an accident he had survived the summer before his senior year at Whitworth College, when he worked in a mine in Montana. He had been eating lunch in an underground break room, facing the door, when an explosion hurled him into the wall. The detonation killed the man across the table. Christian suffered three broken ribs and a chipped elbow bone, and the flash of gas permanently blasted, into the epidermis of his face and palms, infinitesimal particles of sulfur and granite, turning him into an Easter Island face, or the Man in the Iron Mask. Or maybe something more ridiculous.

Weeks after the accident, his girlfriend visited him and, after some initial stiffness between them, she joked he looked like the Tin Man. Christian squeaked through locked jaws, "Oil can!" They laughed at this. He was so touched by her loyalty, he cried after she left. He had never really understood her character until it had been put to the test. A week later he received a tear-blotted letter saying she wanted to break up. It wasn't about his face, he mustn't think that. She'd had doubts already. Maybe what happened to him just crystallized something she'd always known about his personality: metallic, stony, uncommunicative. She didn't mean to be cruel; she hoped they could remain friends, but it was only fair to let him know in the clearest possible terms why she was doing this. Otherwise he would think she was reacting to a superficial matter like appearance.

So he liked Chicago, where only the panhandlers looked at your face (and they sympathetically, hungrily, so that after handing out three or four dollars, he learned to ignore them), and though he knew he was violating some unwritten code of urban behavior, he made use of the opportunity to eye the women.

Everywhere he saw attractive young females, many of whom apparently took pleasure in the gazes of men on their bare bellies; this had been the fashion when Christian was in middle school, and he was torn between delight at its return and affront at a style whose intent was to tantalize men with no hope of reward. It frankly surprised him how many stout young women were willing to expose their potbellies, as capacious as longshoremen's, but one also saw many slender and beautiful tummies.

The sensations of desire and longing followed by despair happened to him several times a day in Chicago. In the morning he would have coffee and a muffin in the hotel restaurant, where he was served by an immigrant from Barbados with a mocking laugh and features like a Mali sculpture, and even though she was forty-five and married and slightly steatopygous, she wore sexy batik skirts that parted to reveal her legs when she crossed the room. In River North, he saw a blonde in high heels walking her dog, and he followed her for a block or two until she began to cast uneasy glances over her shoulder. Three times in his first twenty-four hours in Chicago, he bought a bottle of mineral water at a corner deli on State Street just to see the cashier, a Nepalese girl in a sari.

On his second afternoon in town he found a seat at Kuzmich's, an empty sidewalk café on a leafy street near the Water Tower, and he again fell deeply and passionately in love, this time with a slim Asian waitress who wore leather pants and a blouse that left her midriff bare, so that men could admire the ankh tattooed around her puckered navel. She wore an outlandish pair of dark glasses, pointy-cornered and studded with rhinestones.

Her name was Vicky, and she was working on an MFA in painting at the Art Institute of Chicago. Christian was no expert, but her accent sounded Chinese. She was in her late twenties, and she smiled fetchingly as she brought him a generous splash of Tennessee sour mash whiskey on the rocks in a tumbler shaped like a cube. Christian partook of the golden distillation in minute sips. Sunlight suffused the Midwestern haze and glowed in the wisp of cloud snagged in the snail horns of the Hancock Center, and Christian thereby decreed that all men of all lands heretofore would commemorate this date in July, with whiskey and huzzahs and the celebratory firing of Kalashnikovs into the sky, as the Day of the Navel Ankh.

He really wanted to taste the blue skin around her pink pucker.

Vicky noticed his stare and approached. "Everything all right?"

He tapped his water glass. "Refill, please."

"Sure. You ready for another Jack's, too?"

"I'm still working on this one."

She fetched a pitcher, and as Christian sat there with his arm draped across the back of a chair, she leaned across him to fill his glass, suffusing the air with a floral perfume and the faint odor of her sweat, and her belly, the holy ankh itself, came within a quarter inch of his forearm. A faint trail of down on her tummy electrified his arm hair.

"Oops!" she said.

"Sorry," Christian said, though he had done nothing.

There were few customers at four-thirty in the afternoon, and Vicky was bored and was willing to talk with little urging. Originally from Hong Kong, she had moved to Chicago with her parents twelve years ago. Her full name was Victoria. This interested Christian.

"Isn't that like naming someone from New York 'Brooklyn'?" he said.

"Oh, don't say that; I always hated my name. So have you been to Hong Kong?"

"No, just read about it. This is the first real trip I've taken anywhere in ages, apart from hopping a train. I stopped traveling after college. Thought it would be unfair to terrorize the children of the world."

She did not become awkward, as people usually did when he joked about his appearance. She said, "You hopped a train?"

But just then an egg-shaped couple wearing shorts and Cubs jerseys entered the roped-off area where he was sitting, and Vicky hurried over to seat them.

When she returned with the early dinner he had ordered—a seared pork chop marinated in some kind of spicy sauce—Christian said, "Nice shades."

"Oh, I sort of collect them. These I found in the free box at St. Vincent de Paul. If I don't wear sunglasses I get headaches."

She left so quickly she forgot to grind pepper on his salad. As she came back, she discovered the pepper mill clamped in her armpit. She hesitated, then she strode on.

As the café gradually filled, Vicky busied herself elsewhere, and Christian regretted his oblique reference to his face. He had long known it was poor form, as a carnival freak, to allude to his appearance, and he also knew that the Tin Man (played by Jack Haley with the affected elocution of 1930s Hollywood) was not supposed to make women squirm with his obvious leering. He was teary-eyed and sentimental, a eunuch. For whatever reason, she now monitored his lust from afar. He knew that staring could do him no good at all, but he was addicted to Vicky. Her name itself seemed sexual. He wanted to Vickify her, but gently and tenderly, following lengthy foreplay and whispered endearments. He clearly envisioned a scene that he was convinced actually happened in her bedroom last night, as she knelt naked on a modern Swedish wood-framed, queen-size bed in a white-walled room. She was reaching for a jar of cold cream on the nightstand. She worked it into her hands.

Stop it. Women enjoyed such stares only when they came from men who do not resemble coke plant workers or ink-faced Yakuza crime bosses or street urchins who have fallen into a coal bin: in short, normal men. A Salvadoran teenager wearing a ponytail and a pubic triangle of chin hair came out to collect a tub of dishes, and Vicky made a point of tickling him in response to some wisecrack he made. He set down the tub and grabbed her. O, defilement of all that is sacred, the ankh touched his plastic apron, filthy with spinach and alfredo sauce, before she freed herself. Glancing at Christian, she cleaned the goo from her tummy with a napkin, then flung it into the tub. So there.

That night, as he lay in bed, he daydreamed that Vicky invited him to her place for a drink. But some cruel portion of his unconscious waylaid the fantasy by dispatching a crazed murderer to lie in wait for Christian in her stairwell. As Christian reached Vicky's landing, the madman pounced. They grappled on the stairs and came crashing through the door to her floor, and Vicky looked out from her apartment and screamed. The assailant managed to get a Ruger from his pocket. He fired, and a slug tore through the meat and cartilage of Christian's shoulder. Christian somehow ended up with the gun. He fired point-blank through the madman's face.

For some reason, after this he found it impossible to make love to Vicky in his mind.

Why would she be interested in you, anyway? You idiot, you repulsive monster, stop flirting, she doesn't need it. Go look at yourself, get up and go look.

He flipped on the light switch, blinding himself, and stumbled to the bathroom, where he studied his face in the mirror. The sheet-metal mask was as elastic as leather, it contorted with anger, the white teeth flashed in his mouth. "Tin Man," he scoffed. "Stop it. Stop it. Stop it. *Stop it.*" By which he meant, "Stop hoping," or maybe, "Stop falling in love."

Or perhaps he just wanted Vicky to stop tormenting him.

■ Christian returned the next day to Kuzmich's, and the day after that, arriving each time in the afternoon, before the dinner crowd, and Vicky would seat him at a pleasant table in the shade with a view of a church down the street. She sat at the next table over and folded napkins. She always wore sunglasses—Tuesday's pair had yellow frames, Wednesday's were sleek and black. He sometimes saw her looking at him with a questioning expression. He smiled. She shrugged.

On Thursday, she was wearing a short skirt, and high on her inner thigh he noticed a dark spot, which he at first mistook for a bruise and then recognized as a scar. Had she been stabbed? Wasn't there an artery in that region? Perhaps Vicky had a hard side; it was not impossible that she had braved an assault at the hands of a rough, good-looking, intoxicating male of the sort women thought they preferred over self-loathing monsters like Christian, until the brutes pulled a knife. Somehow this embittered him.

"What are you staring at?" she asked.

When he blushed, he turned a dusty grape color. He did not know what to say.

"So is this your vacation?" she said. "I mean, you're here every afternoon."

"Oh, I just came to town for a convention, which I'm mostly ditching. Insurance. I'm leaving day after tomorrow. But I like Chicago; I'm thinking of moving here."

"What about all your girlfriends?" she said.

"I don't have any girlfriend."

"Somehow I thought you were taken. I don't know why I had that impression."

"Must have been my good looks."

"Modest, aren't we?"

"Who wouldn't be with a face like this?"

Her mouth fell open, and she began laughing. "Well, you've got a healthy ego, I'll say that."

"Yeah, right."

As he paid his bill, she said, "I'm getting off at six tomorrow. You want me to show you the sights before you leave?"

— They had agreed to meet beside the Tribune Tower, where the paper had sealed within its walls stones from the Pyramids of Giza, the Taj Mahal, Angkor Wat, the White House. As Christian approached, Vicky stood whistling at the stone from Colonel Robert McCormick's house, and the breeze carried the tune to him. She pursed her lips and blew deliberately, like a child still mastering the skill, and her artlessness made him feel tender and protective. She wore not leather or a miniskirt, but jeans and a green blouse and a nylon backpack, yet she nevertheless conveyed an impression of stylishness. Perhaps it was her sunglasses (Do you wear them when you make love? he wondered), or the many rings on her fingers and thumbs.

She felt his approach and turned to him.

"Well, it's God's gift to women."

"Nice to see you too, Vicky."

She curtsied. "Just giving you a hard time."

A realization hit that caused him to break out in a sweat, for he became certain that Vicky's sunglasses were preventing her from seeing the color of his skin.

"I don't have much time, though," he said. "An hour at most."

"An hour? What, are you crazy? I thought your plane left tomorrow."

"I just have to get back to my room and pack for tomorrow."

"Oh, come on. Just stuff everything in your suitcase tomorrow morning. So, have you tried one of those architectural tours on the river? I hear they're actually rather interesting."

━ On the lower deck they bought plastic cups of syrah at a bar, and then they went upstairs to sit in the rows of chairs facing a tour guide with a microphone. He was a college kid who had spent his summer polishing a bitter shtick involving eyerolling and sarcasm. ("Got any Cheeseheads here? Well, you can just jump in the lake and swim home. Just kidding. You know I love Wisconsin. And, hey, thanks for sending your sewage our way.") Vicky dragged Christian back to the aft rail. Nearby stood a fat man with capillaries embroidered on his chin and cheeks and a wart at the corner of his eye. He rocked back and forth and muttered, "Fuck! Fuck! Fuck!" The man, whose name seemed to be Watkins, spoke in two voices, his own and a frightful croak, and Christian would have found the situation comical had his entire demeanor not suggested the terror and entrapment of the mentally ill. "It's all the same thing," he said, and the voice replied, "Oh, no, it's not; you're a piece of shit, Watkins, and you know it. No one ever gave a flying rat's ass about you." A little boy nearby mimicked the voice, inhaling as he spoke, "Flying rat's ass, flying rat's ass."

But his mother, a lank-haired woman who sat nearby with her "Naked Co-ed Volleyball" T-shirt hitched up to suckle an infant at a nipple the color and circumference of a Safeway tomato, told him to shut up. Then she called to Watkins, "Look, mister, some of us got kids here, and we don't appreciate that kind of language."

Watkins started, then headed downstairs to the bar.

"Sad," Christian said.

"It's horrible," Vicky said. "I know a guy—Pete's his name—who's an absolutely brilliant artist, but he ended up in prison after he stabbed me. I mean ruthlessly. Tried to stab me in a place you don't even want to think about. He was schizophrenic. He still writes to me sometimes."

"Was he your boyfriend?"

She raised her hands, let them fall. "Sort of."

"Aren't you afraid of this guy? I mean, when he gets out?"

"He's in for seven years, but he says he plans to look me up afterward. He sends me love poetry that he composes in a prison writing workshop. Doggerel, I found, but supposedly the instructor thinks he's a genius. Some of it was quite personal, about us. Also violent. He used to be a normal guy, you know."

Their conversation, as they headed down the river and back through the locks into the harbor, was unmemorable. Not that it was dull, but he was distracted by the worry that she might remove her sunglasses, and he was also drunk on the elixir of her presence, on being with a woman who was beautiful and had blue paint under her nails and had left the top two buttons of her blouse undone, affording a glimpse of her flowered white bra with a clasp of the sort that unhooked in front. In his mind he undid it with his teeth. Vicky had seen the same show of Flemish triptychs that he had stumbled across at an art museum downtown. He knew nothing about art and had not for a long time been a man of faith, but the paintings somehow awakened in him a need to believe in a God who would, in the afterlife, grant him a radiant new self.

Christian would later remember the small dramas between them that assumed greater significance, like a war between two anthills rendered Napoleonic by the perspective of a nature cinematographer lying in the dust: his hand crept toward hers on the rail, then he checked himself, fearing she would find his proximity distasteful. She adjusted her earring and then set her hand down again so close to his he could almost feel its warmth. He wanted to finger the bracelet she wore, just to add the sensation of jade to his catalog of memories of this evening, but he was afraid to break the barrier between them. Instead, he jabbed at it childishly with an index finger and offered a bland compliment: "Nice bracelet." It was a Buddhist amulet, she said, but Vicky was not Buddhist but a lapsed Mormon.

She took his hand and stroked his thumb with her fingers. Anyone looking at them might mistake them for a couple.

Yet he felt guilty and tried to devise an escape—perhaps he should dive into the river, climb out on the opposite bank, and vanish into the crowd. He let her hand go.

"Clammy," she said.

"Mine?"

"No, mine."

"Not true."

Then, from the harbor, they watched the sun sink to the level of the skyscraper tops. The moment was coming, he was sure. Sooner or later she would remove her sunglasses.

Remember this moment. Remember her look of attraction, not the look of disgust that is coming. Remember her heart-shaped mouth and the face that is delicate and flat and porcelain in appearance. Remember the way she smiles in two parts, first the left side, then, more reluctantly, the right. Remember her happy look as she stares at the city.

"I've never gone on one of these tours before," Vicky said. "Kind of fun, if it weren't for the twit on the microphone. That sky is so luminous. Even if it's only the air pollution that makes it so beautiful."

"You should've seen the sunsets in Spokane the summer after Mount St. Helen blew. Nineteen eighty. I was a kid."

All that mattered was that she keep her sunglasses on until they docked; then he could ditch her. But, of course, by the time they disembarked he wanted more of her. And when she said, "Have you seen Millennium Park?" he said, "Show me."

As they walked south on Michigan Avenue, he began wishing, self-destructively, to see her eyes, but really, sooner or later, it would happen. Perhaps he should just seize the initiative himself. Find a pleasant but rather dusky bar, where the dimness would mute the shock. John Merrick in shadows. Remove her sunglasses, gaze into her dark eyes, and in his most sonorous and romantic tones, squeak, "Oil can!" Oh, ha, ha, ha, how they would laugh in a daze of happy desire at the realization that looks don't matter! It's what's in the heart that counts! But really, he knew she would be furious, mostly at herself, for having wasted an evening with a charity case.

Then again, he thought, shrugging inwardly, the light was fading. Soon, as darkness fell, she would remove her sunglasses, and the night would reveal that which had been hidden to her.

The park was crowded and smelled of corn dogs and sweat, and the pavement by the café was sticky where someone had spilled a milkshake. The climate was humid enough to be Africa. Christian's shirt was damp, and he mopped his face with his handkerchief. Vicky appeared unaffected. They admired the distorted reflections of the skyscrapers on a metallic bean the size of an asteroid and studied the twin columns of glass bricks where giant video-image faces (sometimes with acne or crooked teeth) smiled, puckered, and then spat water on the swarms of children who squealed and splashed on the pavement below.

Christian said, "Why did they choose such odd faces to film, I wonder?"

"You're so fixated on appearances."

At that moment a gasp arose from the crowd to their right, and Watkins—the madman from the boat—came lunging toward them. He bumped Vicky, and Christian cried, "Hey, watch it!" Watkins did not notice. A man in a U.S. Marines T-shirt lunged after him and rode him like a steer to the ground. Pinning the madman's arms to his chest, the Marine began punching. Watkins thrashed and squirmed free and tried to crawl away, but the Marine grabbed his leg, nearly pulling his trousers off.

The Marine straddled Watkins and drew back to slug him again. Lunging forward, Christian caught the fist.

Even in the middle of a fight, the Marine's face registered incredulity at the gray face confronting him.

Christian said, "Leave him alone."

"Back off, pal. He called my wife a bitch."

"He doesn't know what he's saying. Can't you see he's sick?"

"Do you know him?"

"He's just a crazy old man."

"Well, then, fuck off."

Watkins's nose was bleeding, and his eyes rolled back in his head. The Marine tried to yank his hand free. Christian held on.

True, Christian lifted weights, jogged on a treadmill four days a week, had lettered in wrestling in high school; but he was not a fighter, and his opponent disengaged himself from Watkins and head-butted Christian in the face. Something crunched, and he nearly blacked out. Christian found himself beneath the burly kid, who hesitated, as if unsure whether his wife's honor demanded that he beat up this meddler as well. Using a wrestling move, Christian rolled onto his hands and knees and hooked an arm around the Marine's leg, pulling him off, but this left his face vulnerable to the drubbing that the Marine, as if motion-activated, began to issue. Vicky grabbed the Marine, and a loose elbow smacked her head. In the corner of Christian's vision appeared a pair of pointy-toed, lace-topped cowboy boots. They began kicking him.

Then a cop loomed over them, spraying the perps with Cap-stun until they fell apart weeping.

━ Several witnesses attested that Christian was only trying to stop an attack on some poor kook, and the cop let him and Vicky go and arrested the Marine for assault and disorderly conduct. It was dark by the time Christian and Vicky began strolling north on Michigan Avenue. Watkins had been picked up by a supervisor at the group home where he lived. Christian cooled his throbbing nose with ice wrapped in a paper towel. His entire body was sore.

"How you doing?" Vicky said.

"I'm going to sue: he ruined my nose."

"You poor thing."

On the bridge over the river, she stopped him and ran two fingers around his swollen nose, over his cheeks and lips. He closed his eyes and savored the touch, the circling, the fingertips smoothing his eyebrow. Strike any blow, batter my face and my body, only heal me with your fingers afterward. He felt a warm breeze. She was blowing on his eye.

"Does that hurt?"

"No, no. 'Hurt' is not the word I would use."

"You're crying, this one eye."

Christian wiped his eye on his shoulder and smeared a bloody epaulet there. "It still stings from the pepper spray. How about you? It looked like he really clocked you with that flying elbow."

"Oh, it was just a thump on the head. What hurt was when his wife bit me."

"You're kidding."

Vicky showed him the dents on her wrist.

"I wonder if she's had her distemper shot."

As the ice melted, Christian tasted iron and water. He squeezed the paper towel over the river. An ice cube squirted out and plopped into the water. From the darkness a gull dove at the sound.

When the time came to remove Vicky's sunglasses, Christian had planned to be romantic, or dramatic, or bravely candid, diminishing himself by revealing that which was necessary, but when he finally worked up the courage to do so, he found himself scolding her.

"I can't believe you're still wearing those dark glasses. How can you see at night?"

"It's bright enough under the lights."

"I want to see your eyes."

"Some other time."

"Come on, I want to show you—I want you to see—"

"Leave me alone!"

But he insisted, and her face hardened. Before he could reach she snatched off her own sunglasses.

Christian had braced himself for her expression of astonishment and loathing; he was not prepared for his own surprise. Her eyes were rather plain, and the left eyeball was mis-set in its socket, peering cross-eyed across the bridge of her nose. She was no longer beautiful. Quite frankly, she looked insane. He did not know what to say. Stupidly he told her, "You're pretty."

"Shut up."

"Well, I mean, look at me."

"What about you?"

"Can't you see? Come here, under the streetlight."

"Christian, what are you—oh, my gosh!"

And that's how Christian knew that Vicky finally saw him, the Tin Man. He told her about the accident as succinctly as possible. He concluded, "My face got in the way."

"You poor thing." Then she began to giggle. "I couldn't tell. Not with these glasses. I didn't understand. I thought you were so full of yourself."

As they looked downriver at the corncob towers of Marina City, Christian thought, A fellow misfit: it figures. Why else would anyone spend an evening with me? He felt he had been the victim of a hoax.

Vicky returned her sunglasses to the bridge of her nose.

"You'll be blind by the time you're thirty-five," he said, "wearing those things at night."

"Men are nicer to me when I wear them."

He snatched the sunglasses and flung them into the river. For an instant she looked like she would cry, then he thought she would slap him, scream at him, call him an arrogant jerk, and he was prepared to respond, to make her understand that even with a face like his he had a right to see who she was, and to be seen. But she suffered the indignity with stoicism, like a fat woman who submits when a stranger on a busy street snatches her ice-cream cone and says, "Do you really need this?"

Then Vicky strode off through the crowd.

Christian lunged after her and grabbed her elbow.

"Let me go!"

"Vicky, look, I'll buy you another pair, okay? I'm sorry, but I did it because—"

She flung his arm away. "You did it because you're an asshole, like everyone else."

Something glittered on her cheeks. Christian pulled her to him, and before kissing her with his purple-gray lips, he told her, "You don't have to hide them, I mean, why would you hide them from me?"

SLAVA

EVERY LIFE, DR. TAMARA RUDYAKOVA BELIEVED, IS DETERMINED BY a few fateful moments comprising but a blip of one's allotted years on this planet. At such times the entire future hangs on the decisions one makes; everything else is mere consequence.

Case in point: a few minutes' conversation with a child beggar one Saturday in late August of 2002, midway through Tamara's third decade, or "halfway to the grave," as a colleague had cheerfully toasted her on her birthday last month. There was a whiff of golden autumn in the air, when the trees yellow on the hills of Vladivostok and whitecaps blossom on the Sea of Japan and the weather, in this gap between the summer typhoons and late October snowfalls, is on its best behavior all year. That afternoon, Tamara was hobbling across the Vtoraya Rechka market, where the produce of the dachas crowded the stalls: onions and carrots and bunches of dill and filthy potatoes the size of a child's fist. An outdoor market is not an easy place to negotiate on crutches on a busy Saturday. She carried her purchases in a daypack slung from her breast to keep thieves from raiding it from behind as she queued, and other shoppers thumped her crutches with their duffel bags as she sculled through the throng. A butcher with an ax hacked a frozen side of beef into pieces, and a flying chip of bone nearly blinded her.

She was halted by the scent of muskmelon. Nearby, a Korean farmer sat on a stool beside a pyramid of cantaloupes buzzing with gnats. From one of them he gouged out a wedge for a woman to sample. Tamara could almost taste the hot sweet summer flesh of the fruit. Perhaps she could fit a cantaloupe in her pack, but did she really want to lug it, along with everything else, up the hill and five flights of stairs to her apartment on Kirova? So she stood there for a moment and simply savored the smell, reluctant to surrender the associations of youth, of a time when she was able to walk without crutches, of the collective farm where in Soviet times university students had been compelled to help with the harvest and where she had made love, for the first time, to her ex-husband, Filipp, then a fellow medical student. But then, having detained her, fate drew her gaze toward a small boy sitting by the entrance to the corrugated steel building that housed the clothing market.

Strange to say, his face alone set her heart pounding. He had long-lashed eyes, pursed lips, an upturned nose, and ears that were pinched inward at the top. He appeared to be a rather small five, and in his jeans and "Star Wars" T-shirt, he was as grubby as the homeless Roma and Tajiks who passed through the city every summer. Yet with his blond hair, sunburnt face, and blue-gray eyes, he had the same Petersburg complexion as Tamara herself. Propped beside him was a cardboard sign decorated with an icon of an infant Christ and the Mother of God, along with the words, "IN THE NAME OF CHRIST, KIND PEOPLE, SPARE SOME CHANGE FOR AN ORPHAN." The boy had aroused the pity of other shoppers, it seemed, for he had accumulated a small pile of coins and ruble notes in a candy box, to the envy of a babushka panhandler nearby, who cursed him and told him to go find another place to beg, this was her spot. But he ignored her, his attention was elsewhere. A few meters away, a woman was selling pit bull puppies from a cardboard box, and the boy was riling them by tossing pebbles at them while their mistress was preoccupied chatting with a friend. He threw with his left hand.

His right hand was hidden in his pocket, but even before he pulled it out, Tamara knew with a sickening prescience what she would see: his thumb and forefinger were missing. Nevertheless, she gasped when he reached to collect a pebble in his three remaining digits and transferred it to his left hand.

Noticing Tamara, the boy jingled his candy box at her.

As a rule she did not give alms, and indeed beggars scarcely glanced at her, sensing that a cripple would be immune to sympathy for the able-bodied, but to this boy she handed a hundred rubles, his largest note of the day.

"What's your name?"

"Azamat."

"Has anyone ever called you Slava?"

"No."

"Where do you live?"

"In Moscow, but we're staying in Vladivostok for the summer. Me and my mama."

"I thought you were an orphan."

He shrugged. The sign, after all, was only a prop.

"Where's your mama?"

"Over there."

"Who, in the red jeans?"

"No, way over there, sitting."

At a busy crossroads in the market, a dark Caucasian woman in a long skirt and kerchief sat with her hand extended, having staked out a different place to beg.

"You don't look like her."

He did not know what to say. He threw another pebble.

"Stop it, they're nice doggies," Tamara said. "What about your papa?"

"He died in a car accident."

"I see. So, how long will you be sitting here?"

Belatedly suspicious of her questions, he fell silent and stared.

"Because I might buy you a little toy. Would you like a toy?"

"A soldier."

"Then I'll come back with a soldier. But I need to know how long you'll be here."

"Until closing."

"And tomorrow?"

"Mama says we're staying through September, *inshallah*."

Inshallah. The word, with its implication of obeisance to a God scarcely able to contain His infinite wrath against the cockroach race He had created, was a sarcoma on the lips of the child. Outside the market, Tamara flagged down a car (a luxury borne of urgency; she usually traveled by streetcar or bus) and went straight to the Sovetsky Rayon precinct station on Stoletiya Avenue. She was a medical doctor, now employed as a pharmacist because the pay was better, but she was afraid the police would not take her seriously in her shabby weekend clothes: a youngish harpy in frayed jeans and windbreaker. Her face, once pretty if a little too broad and angular, was now haggard, in her view: the skin growing ruddy, her eyes bloodshot, her left cuspid of gold. Thank God, she at least had worn makeup.

Lieutenant Farid Yengalychev, the duty officer, was a Tatar with Mongolian eyes and a moustache that curled into the corners of his mouth, and she found him filling out a report on which she glimpsed the phrase, "stabbing the victim repeatedly with his hypodermic needle." He heard her out with a mournful solicitude. One would think a man who dealt with rape and murder and mafia car bombs would no longer be moved by any particular tale of woe, but he sighed, "Oi," as if oppressed by her story, and promised to investigate. Unfortunately, the precinct was too short-staffed to follow up today. President Putin was in town to meet with what's-his-name, the North Korean president, and every spare man had been called up for security—right, Kim, the Dear Leader: that was it. Tomorrow, he said, after Kim headed back home in his armored train, they would be able to look into this.

"We can't wait till tomorrow! They might be gone."

"If they've been here all month, they won't pack up and leave overnight."

Tamara caught a bus back to the market, still lugging her groceries, only to find the gates closed for the evening.

She returned to the tenement apartment she had inherited from her mother. The public spaces were filthy, with puddles of urine in the lift and smears of fishheads and dog feces tracked up the stairwell, but in the refuge of her apartment, she boiled *pelmeni* for dinner and opened a bottle of semidry Moldavian red wine. After two glasses she phoned Filipp, who was with the Red Cross in Moscow. They had not spoken in three years, and when he answered, she nearly hung up. She greeted him, and he sounded wary. Or perhaps he no longer recognized her voice. His had changed, too; it had roughened, as if smoking and ordering about the staff in his ward had dulled the warm oboe tones that used to penetrate her ear canal when he murmured to her as they made love. He began coughing.

"You sound sick," she said.

"It's nothing. A little bronchitis. What's up?"

But as soon as Tamara described what she had seen, Filipp cried out in a strangled voice, "No, no, no, no, no, I don't want to hear this."

"Filipp, listen."

"No, you listen. Why would you call me with this foolishness? You know he's dead. Have you been drinking?"

In the background a woman asked, "Who is it?" and Filipp pressed the receiver against his ribcage to muffle the sound, though it had the opposite effect; it made Tamara feel as if she were lying atop him with her cheek on his hairy chest. "Can't you wait till I'm off the goddamned phone?" he said. He had never spoken to Tamara like that—at least not until the end.

He returned to say, "Tamara, don't do this to yourself, to me. I can't take it, I really can't."

She heard an infant crying somewhere in Filipp's apartment.

"Do you have a baby, Filipp?"

"Yes." He seemed reluctant to say more, but she waited. "Two kids. Boy and a girl."

"Why didn't you let me know? How old are they?"

"He's almost three, and she's eleven months, already. Hard to believe. I don't know, I wasn't sure how to tell you. I thought it would remind—. They're so adorable, though. Yesterday, Lyuba stood up and walked three steps like a drunken sailor and then plopped down on her bottom. She's been creeping around holding the furniture, but this was the first time on her own. The boy didn't walk until he was thirteen months."

"Congratulations. I'm so glad for you; you were always a good papa."

"Thank you." He did not return the compliment. She would not have allowed it if he had.

"Oh, Filya. This boy today in the market—"

"Tamara, even if he were alive, you couldn't possibly recognize him."

"I know, I know, it's ridiculous. But I did, I knew him. He even has your ears."

Somehow this got him. "Tamarochka, why are you torturing yourself? There's not a night that goes by that I don't lie awake thinking about our poor little guy. But you yourself saw the video—"

Then Filipp began coughing so hard he could not speak. He croaked, "Good-bye," and hung up.

After that, the silence in her apartment began to oppress her, and Tamara fitted a Maria Callas record on her old phonograph. The needle spooled the grooves and squawked about dust and former mishandling; then Callas's pure voice filled the room, vibrating within the concrete walls:

> *Vissi d'arte, vissi d'amore,*
> *non feci mai male ad anima viva!*
> *Con man furtiva,*
> *quante miserie conobbi, aiutai.*

Balancing herself with her crutches, Tamara mounted a stool in the kitchen, rummaged about in the storage cabinet that extended over the hall ceiling, and retrieved a cardboard box, which she opened up on the table. It contained a videocassette, an envelope, and three tiny sets of baby clothes that she had been unable to bring herself to throw away. The cassette she left in the box, but she got out the envelope and laid out the outfits, which had feet attached and even, on the blue suit, little mittens so the baby would not scratch his face. She fingered the soft flannel. Then after refilling her glass (her third, she would have sworn, had it not been for the evidence of the empty bottle with its residue, like maroon coffee grounds, around the punt) and fortifying it with a shot of Zolotoi Rog, she opened the envelope.

Inside was a birth certificate ("RUDYAKOV, Vyacheslav Filippovich. Nalchik, Russia. 6th May 1997") and twenty-four photographs taken inside the apartment she and Filipp had shared in Nalchik, in the Caucasus. She could see the clock and the carpet hung on the wall, the glass-fronted bookshelves decorated with the portrait of Pushkin clipped from a newspaper. In some, Filipp was holding the baby; in others, it was Tamara, still bloated after her pregnancy, but so young and beautiful just five years ago (is it possible she had considered herself plain then?). She studied Slava's face, with his chipmunk cheeks and Asian eyes and the pugilistic nose of a newborn. He was asleep in most of the shots, but in two of them he stared at the photographer, in this case Filipp, with the disinterested gaze of an infant monkey, clutching Tamara's blouse in his tiny fists, as if not trusting his own mother to hold onto him. He used to cry when she handed him to Filipp.

Suddenly she threw everything back in the box and hurled it into the corner. Stupid fucking superstitious old hag, witch, worthless scum, vermin, swine, bitch. *Devil* take you, *devil* take you, *devil* take you.

It occurred to her that she was saying all this aloud, screaming it, in fact, while inexplicably stressing the name of the Archfiend. She twisted the stylus right off the phonograph, snapped the record in half, threw it all, along with her wine glass, out the window, and then retreated to the other room and fell onto the bed, sobbing. After a fitful slumber of an hour or so she woke up with a headache and did not sleep again until dawn.

■ What else, Tamara asked herself as she lay in the dark, would she include on the short list of those moments that changed everything? Certainly the invitation to walk along Lake Khanka with Filipp that night at the collective farm when she had really been looking for Zhorik. (This was long before the injury that crippled her.) But the others had gone off to Kamen-Rybalov to drink in an abandoned military barracks—roofless, rubble-strewn, and filled with shattered bottles and hypodermic needles— and so she found Filipp reading alone in the men's quarters. "You want to go for a walk?" Filipp asked. "I'm going blind reading in here." It was the uncertainty in his voice, the suggestion that he was prepared for a refusal and would not have blamed her for it, that caused her to agree. In the dark, as they followed a cow path along a berm between two rice paddies, she had not been able to see his plain face with its large nose and thick lips, and she was attracted to his deep voice, shy intelligence, and evangelical passion for the cello (she had known nothing about classical music). On Lake Khanka a waxing moon splintered the surface into glittering shards through which the black forms of Chinese fishing boats came creeping into Russian waters, and she had let him kiss her. Somehow (remembering it still amazed her, still melted her) they ended up skinny-dipping together.

Add to that the moment, six years later, when Filipp came home to their apartment in Vladivostok to announce that there was a Red Cross office in Nalchik that needed a doctor and was promising a generous salary to someone willing to travel on occasion to Chechnya. And certainly she would include the instant whose exact timing she would never know, in which Slava was conceived. When she missed her period, and the nausea and goldfish flutters began inside her, she had nearly decided to abort the parasite within. Filipp agreed that it was the wrong time to exchange their lifestyle for what he described as a life of "diapers and two-liter jars of mayonnaise and rushing kids to and from daycare every morning and evening."

Tamara was then earning meager wages as a surgeon at Respublika Hospital, but Filipp's dollar-based salary afforded them an apartment, a new television, an occasional bottle of Italian wine, and even a vacation in Cyprus the previous summer. Besides, she had her patients to think about, such as the nine-year-old boy brought into surgery with a gasket in his brain, the victim of a Chechen car bombing at a market in Nalchik, and she had seen him through surgery and a coma to the point where he was learning to speak and might even walk again. But even if she believed that an embryo was not yet a person, she could not bring herself to abort this soul-in-waiting, since her rights as a woman had to be weighed against the future perspective of a child who would take being and consciousness for granted and never guess that Mama had once considered purging him from the great chain of being. For few of us, she thought, however hard our lot, would decline the win in the orgasmic lottery that brings us, against trillionfold odds, into the universe's most elite club, comprising those congregations of molecules which possess sight, hearing, touch, taste, self-knowledge, love, and despair.

Once she had been backed into the decision to have a child, it was surprisingly easy to about-face and embrace the notion. Filipp, too, came around; he began to say he wanted a girl after an older colleague told him, "Girls love their papas more than boys do," yet for this very reason she knew that fate would bring her a boy. She no longer remembered the girls' names they had considered, but if it was to be a boy, they had agreed on Vyacheslav, after her late father, a researcher at the Pacific Oceanological Institute who had died of a heart attack on a scientific cruise to Vietnam when she was fourteen and had been returned in a refrigerated hold for burial in Vladivostok. Besides, she liked the nickname "Slava," which meant *glory*. The formation of a human being inside her was a miracle to which she contributed nothing, unless you counted becoming a teetotaler for the duration of the pregnancy—hardly a sacrifice since at that time she had drunk no more often than once a month anyway, and as a doctor she had examined children with fetal alcohol syndrome disorders, with their deformed sternums, webbed toes, flattened philtra, and eyes that would not move in the same direction.

━ *Glory.* Tamara was becoming acquainted with her son long before the allotted nine months were up. He had ticklish feet: when he thrust his soles against the wall of her abdomen, she would scratch at the bulge and make him wriggle inside. He disliked loud noises and kept recoiling during the week that workmen spent knocking down a wall and building a counter in Tamara's ward. He woke at eleven every night and passed the dark hours kick-boxing, as if practicing to defend himself against foes he would be encountering outside the womb. Filipp would lie snoring beside her in bed, and as she lay on her side with a pillow between her knees, she sought wisdom in the suffering of sleeplessness. Sometimes it became too much to take, and she cried. Filipp would wake and murmur, "Poor girl," and massage her back. But then he slipped back into slumber, and she was left alone with Slava and his fierce inner sambo.

The contractions began one morning on a day when she was off work, and she called the Red Cross and left a message for Filipp, who was out, and caught a bus to the maternity home. After four hours of agony the baby appeared, purple, with a white umbilical cord hanging from his tummy; his testicles were swollen from hydrocele. "What a little stud you are," the nurse said. The doctor suctioned his mouth and slapped his bottom, and poor Slava, not knowing what awaited him, drew his first breath and wailed. Tears rolled down Tamara's cheeks. As the nurse washed his tiny form, Tamara kept saying, "I want my baby, I want my baby." Then at last he was wriggling in her arms. But when Slava latched onto her breast, it felt as if strings were being threaded through her nipples, and the joy of his birth dissolved into a strange feeling of despair. Strings and despair: these would always be her sensations when nursing, during the three weeks she had a baby.

That evening, she joined the other new mothers at the third-story windows facing the street. Down below, Filipp stood among the fathers and other family members who, forbidden from entering, had gathered in the parking lot to wave. She held Slava close to her and turned his tiny, capped head so that Filipp could see. She knew that a newborn sees only blurry shapes, and at distances of no more than thirty-five centimeters;

nevertheless, she said, "It's Papa, look, it's your handsome, brave, wonderful papa, and you'll be just like him." Down below, Filipp was wiping his eyes. He had brought a bag of food for her—dried salmon and black bread and canned pâté—and he grandly waved a bouquet of pink roses as if signaling to low-flying aircraft. On the pavement he had followed the lead of past generations of fathers and slopped a greeting with a can of paint and a brush: "I LOVE YOU TAMARA."

■ The most recent of these fated moments (most recent, that is, until the encounter with the boy in the market) occurred because she had cleaved like a peasant to an old superstition that no one but close family should see a baby in its first month. Slava was twenty-two days old when Tamara, who had taken the year off on maternity leave, discovered they were out of diapers. It was the end of May. The afternoon was sunny and mild, and tiny leaves were pushing forth from the sticky buds on the trees. She swaddled the baby and placed him in his carriage for a brief outing to the store in the basement of an apartment block down the hill. He fell asleep in the elevator on the way down from their floor.

At the top of the steps to the market she hesitated. The only person in sight was a babushka with a Hero Mother of the Soviet Union medal pinned to her coat. She sat on a bench under a maple and cracked sunflower seeds in her teeth, spitting the husks at her elephantine feet. Slava's face, shaded by the canopy, was composed in a sage, almost Confucian expression of peace and trust. Tamara didn't want to lift him out and wake him, and she saw no point in lugging the whole carriage down the steps when she wanted to buy only one item, a package of diapers. Besides, she knew the clerk had a cold and would end up coughing all over the baby as she cooed over him.

And while Tamara did not really believe in old wives' tales, she also felt, like all Russians, that it was folly to ignore them. Even physicists and medical doctors knocked on wood and spat three times over their left shoulder to ward off the devil, and journalists were known to walk around the block to avoid a black cat. The babushka smiled and waved with a sunflower seed pinched between her thumb and index finger, as if to say, Go on, I'll keep an eye on him. Somehow this almost episcopal gesture seemed to grant a dispensation for a brief commitment of her son into the arms of a loving God and His saintly old servant, who had mothered ten offspring of her own. Besides, as even the police and reporters and Tamara's mother-in-law would later concede, back in Soviet times mothers had routinely left their babies in carriages outside stores while they shopped, and nobody would have dreamed of kidnapping an innocent.

Yet when Tamara returned two minutes later, carrying the package of diapers and a bottle of ketchup, the carriage was there, as was the babushka, still spitting seeds, but Slava was gone.

It was memories of that day that awoke her with a start the night after she saw Azamat in the market. She recalled the nightmare that followed the kidnapping: how she screamed, "Who took my baby? Grandma, who took my baby?" while the old woman, once she was made to understand what Tamara was talking about, said, "Why, his mother took him; she went that-a-way." How Tamara dropped the diapers and ketchup and sprinted down the hill in the direction the babushka pointed, onto the crowded sidewalks on Ulitsa Leninskaya, where she grabbed passersby by the coat and cried, "Have you seen a woman with a baby? Somebody just stole my baby." How one man must have thought she was mad when she seized his arm, and with a frightened expression he flung her to the sidewalk (the detective she found at the precinct station kept glancing at her oddly and finally handed her a handkerchief and said, "It's clean. Your chin. You're dripping blood all over your blouse"). How the detective and a police colonel, who was called in from home for this case, kept shaking their heads as if marveling at her stupidity, and she did not contest this, but couldn't they please, please for Christ's sake find her baby?

And there were other memories that still came many times a week in the form of panic attacks: how Filipp sobbed with his face in his hands that afternoon, and then he was compelled to spend the next morning answering the questions of the reporters who showed up at their door, telling them his wife was in despair and on sedatives and could not handle the press right now. Yes, everyone understood, the poor woman (she could hear their sympathetic murmurs through the crescent-shaped cluster of holes punched in the steel outer door), and not that they wished to be insistent, but maybe their story could generate publicity that might help them recover the boy. But then as they departed, a woman reporter stopped to ask, "But what the devil was she thinking?" and Filipp gave up trying to defend her and said, "I don't know, I don't know."

The police told her to watch for a ransom note, and they said this would not necessarily be a bad sign; it would show that the kidnapper was not a maniac or beggar but a criminal with rational aims, such as money. The letter arrived two days after the first round of stories ran in the local papers. There was also a photograph of Slava wailing, his eyes terrified. When she read it, the color of blood oranges pulsed in her field of vision, and she nearly fainted on the black concrete floor by the mailboxes and garbage chute.

In the name of Allah, Most Merciful, Most Gracious!

Praise Allah, the Lord of the Worlds, peace and blessing be to His Prophet Mohammed, who created man so that He could be worshipped alone, so no companions are ascribed to Him, and He permitted jihad on His straight way, so that the Earth could be cleansed of unbelief, infidels, Russian dogs, and their whelps, *inshallah*. For did not Allah say, "Make war on them until no more temptation remains" (Anfal 39)?

As for the hunk of Russian meat known as "Slava" which you are bawling [about] in the media, he will be returned safe if you and the terrorist Russian state meet our conditions. Otherwise he will come home in pieces. First, $25,000 by midnight on 6 June. Second, Russian crusaders and storm troopers must grant independence to all Islamic lands of the Caucasus and Tatarstan by 6 June midnight.

Allah is Our Master!!! and there is no help other than from Him.

Allah Akbar!

God is Greatest!

P.S. Hang a red towel or shirt on your balcony to signify you have received this. Payment instructions will follow.

The political demands were absurd and beyond their powers to grant; likewise, twenty-five thousand was more than Filipp made in a year, and Tamara's small ruble salary as a surgeon at Respublika Hospital, unpaid for eleven months now, was hardly worth mentioning. They had just spent most of their savings, fifteen thousand dollars, to buy the two-room apartment where they lived, and all that was left was a thousand in twenties, which they kept in an envelope behind the encyclopedia on the bookshelf. For two days, Filipp called everyone they knew to beg for money; and although most of their friends were doctors who, like Tamara, were months overdue on their pay, he managed to collect promises for another sixteen hundred dollars.

That evening he sat on the bed for a long time playing sections from Haydn's *Concerto in C Major for Violoncello and Orchestra* and then Shostakovich's *Cello Concerto No. 1*, pausing periodically to swig strong beer, bottle after bottle. She sat, wrapped in a shawl, in a rocking chair next to the crib, and stared out the window at the entry to the basement store where Slava had been stolen, as if she expected the kidnapper to return and lay him on the bench where the babushka had sat. The sunset blazed on the hills, then gradually faded. As darkness fell, she could not drive from her mind the newspaper stories she had read about the emaciated children liberated or ransomed from Chechen kidnappers. It seemed as if a row of child slaves were smudging the balcony window with their faces as they peered in: the toddler who, after a year in a private dungeon, screamed whenever she saw someone in camouflage and kept trying to climb into a wardrobe to sleep every night, the eleven-year-old who weighed fifteen kilos and had become like a wolf after three years with his hands tied behind his back, using his teeth to pick up his dinner plate, biting his relatives, lacking the capacity to speak any language—"like Mowgli, like a child raised by animals," his uncle told reporters. For the first two days she had milked herself and kept it in jars in the refrigerator, but today she did not even bother. Her breasts hurt and there was a bulge in her armpit where the milk was collecting. She was still bleeding from childbirth. When she went to the toilet, she discovered that her drunken husband had pissed all over the seat and the floor, but this was irrelevant to the whereabouts of her baby and she lacked the moral standing to yell at him about it. She cleaned up herself and returned to her vigil.

After a time, Filipp lay his cello and bow on the bed. He paced the room, bumping into furniture and bookcases. Then, without warning, her husband of seven years—passionate lover, musician who played in an amateur string quartet, physician who would with soothing fingers attend to limbs damaged by car bombs or artillery fragments—staggered over and yanked Tamara to her feet by the hair.

"Har could you?" (He was slurring his words.) "Har could you leave a bearby alone? What's a mare with you? What's! A! Mare! With! You!"

When after a time some sober remnant of his consciousness awoke to what he was doing (*yank-yank, yank-yank!*), he let her go and stumbled into the bedroom that had been intended for Slava once he was old enough to sleep by himself. The door slammed and he remained out of sight for the night, appearing only once, after three, to urinate again on the bathroom floor and forage in the kitchen for something to eat.

That morning, Filipp did not speak to her or look at her, not even to say good-bye as he left. Nor did he phone her from work, as he had done several times a day since the baby was born and had continued to do, with increasing desperation, after the kidnapping, always asking, "Any news?" and then, dully, "So how are you holding up?" Tamara again met with police and phoned several old high-school and university classmates in Vladivostok to beg for money, then spent the afternoon knocking on doors in the neighboring apartment blocks, searching for the babushka; the police had been unable to locate her and still had no eyewitness description of the kidnapper. But there were scores of old women in the area, and nobody could recall one who was a Hero Mother.

In the evening, Filipp returned accompanied by a man named Boris Malofeyev, who had read about their case in the papers and sought Filipp out at work. Malofeyev was a former engineer who used to live in Chechnya and now ran a small foundation that worked for the recovery of hostages. He was a gaunt man with a narrow face and dark irises, and his skin was scarlet with eczema.

Malofeyev drew a folder from his briefcase and showed her a newspaper clipping from *Komsomolskaya Pravda*. It described how he had negotiated the release of a five-year-old Russian boy whom Chechens had seized in Ingushetia and held for a year in a basement.

"I've been working on terrorism and kidnapping issues for six years," Malofeyev said. "I have contacts in Chechnya and Ingushetia who can help us get in touch with the kidnappers. It's a vile business, but they're willing to talk to me because they know me. Some of them used to be my colleagues in Soviet times. Hard to believe."

"Why would you want to help us?" Tamara asked. "What's in it for you?"

"I care about the fate of our Russian hostages, especially the children, that's all. This kidnapping is a moral disgrace, something out of the Dark Ages, and I'm trying to combat it in my small way. Once your child is returned, if you wish to make a small donation to help us carry on our work, that would be appreciated, but I don't do this for the money."

"How can we negotiate with them, anyway?" Tamara asked. "Do they think we're just going to phone up Yeltsin and tell him to hand over the Caucasus and Tatarstan to the terrorists? And surely they understand Filipp's work—he's treating wounded Chechen civilians."

"Tamara, just listen, for once," Filipp told the floor.

An awkward pause followed this.

"It's a good question," Malofeyev said. "As I told your husband earlier, you needn't worry about the political demands. That's just window dressing, an attempt to convince themselves that their barbarism is justified because this is God's holy jihad and you are mere infidels. God knows, they don't care about Filipp's medical work with Chechens. The only thing these bastards really understand is money. Kidnapping is a business, that's all. An unspeakably cruel enterprise, yes, but once you accept that, we can proceed rationally and with a reasonable chance of recovering your son."

"But we can't ever come up with the money they're asking. I haven't been paid in months, and even with Filipp's salary, we only have a thousand dollars saved up. We could sell the apartment, but that takes time."

"There's also the eighteen hundred your friends promised."

"Sixteen hundred," Filipp said.

"Whatever. The point is, try to come up with as much as you can. In the meanwhile, I'll put out some feelers. When we find the perpetrators, the negotiations will begin."

"How long does this take?"

"Six months. A year."

"Oh, my God," the Rudyakovs said together.

Filipp glared at her. Then he asked, "What about the deadline?"

"Generally, that's just to pressure you. If you're in contact, you shouldn't have to worry about it."

The police warned them to be careful in dealing with any intermediaries, but detectives had no suggestions on how else to find the baby and limited their investigation to beating up random Chechens they found on the streets. And for his part, Malofeyev was making progress. After several days he reported that the kidnappers were in phone contact with him, and this was confirmed when a new letter arrived, written in the same hand

and Islamist tones as the first, mentioning Malofeyev by name ("tell him not to delay or consequences will be *dire*").

As the deadline approached, they begged from everyone they knew. Filipp's mother sent five hundred dollars (and also phoned in such a rage that Filipp refused to give Tamara the receiver), and his brother and his wife halted a renovation of their apartment and sent their entire savings, more than seven hundred dollars, with a friend who was coming to Nalchik. Tamara's mother wired fifteen hundred rubles through the Post Office, all she had. Old classmates pitched in, and Filipp's colleagues provided a thousand dollars. All told, it brought them to nearly five thousand dollars by June 6.

Malofeyev told them it was best not to make it seem as if the money had been easy to come by, or the scoundrels would simply inflate their demands. Nevertheless, considering Filipp's position on the payroll of a Western organization, they would be lucky if they could reduce the demand to anywhere near five thousand.

"Can't you tell the police whom you're talking to?" Filipp asked.

"I don't know myself. They're the ones who call me. I reached them through my contacts."

"But you can give the names of your contacts to the police."

"If I did, Slava would be in Chechnya the moment the police moved—if he's not there already—and the terrorists would sever their ties to me forever. It's better that we have a way to reach out to them."

As he left, Tamara began to cry, and Malofeyev hesitated, then hugged her.

"Don't worry. Really, your baby isn't such a valuable commodity, and they know it. It's not as if you're oligarchs or members of the army general staff."

He took with him five hundred dollars in good-faith money, and phoned them that night to say he had passed it along to his contact.

Four days later, Tamara found a small box on her doorstep. On the outside was written, "Time's running out." Inside were the severed thumb and forefinger of a baby.

— After this story made the national press, an old friend of her late father's, a former oceanographer who now owned a shipping line in Vladivostok, offered to pay the rest of the twenty-five thousand dollars on the condition they keep his involvement secret. He brought the cash to Moscow during a business trip, and Filipp flew there and met him in Sheremetyevo-1. He returned the same day, and Malofeyev came to their apartment, limping on an ankle he had somehow twisted. "You'll have your baby in your arms before the end of the week," he said. After he left, they watched through the window as he gimped across the courtyard below. He glanced up and seemed to start at the sight of the Rudyakovs, then flashed a thumbs-up. As he headed on, the birches drew closed over him.

It was the last time they ever saw Malofeyev.

After a week, during which there was no answer on his cell phone and the police bawled them out for entrusting their money to someone they hardly knew, Filipp found a second package outside their apartment door, this one containing a videocassette. As he plugged it into the television-video player, a noise escaped Tamara's throat, half sob, half squeak, such as Slava might have made. An Arabic phrase appeared on a black screen, the script golden, three-dimensional, shimmering. Then it cut to a jerky shot of a clearing in a forest where a group of bearded men in camouflage milled about, hoisting Kalashnikovs and a PZRK Strela rocket launcher as they grinned and waved at the camera. They were calling out something, but their voices were indistinct. The video had been filmed at dusk and the quality of the light was poor.

A narrator with a Chechen accent began speaking: "Behold, as the glorious mujahideen extract vengeance against the infidel occupiers and terrorists in our march toward victory, *inshallah*."

He went on for some time in this vein until three Russian civilians—two men and a woman—were marched into the field and forced to kneel, their hands bound behind them.

The narration evolved from polemic into a singsong incantation.

"Allah the Almighty! Allah the Almighty! The call leaves our throats, to fill the Earth with the fragrance of aromatic plants!"

The first hostage was a shaggy grandfather who hunched over as if from a back injury. The narrator began singing in Arabic, in the djinn-like voice that echoes from minarets throughout the House of Islam. A tall mujahid stepped forward, his beard red and right socket a fleshy smudge, as if he were missing an eye—it was hard to tell in the video. He booted the old man between the shoulder blades, flattening him on the ground. The mujahid knelt on the hostage's back while his comrades sat on the arms and legs. Someone handed him an archer's bow, which he leveled on the hostage's neck.

Or no, not a bow. A hacksaw.

The blade cut back and forth and the old man screamed until his vocal cords were severed from behind. Then the tall mujahid held up the head by the ears as the camera's palsied gaze closed in, observed the sightful eyes and the gaping jaw with its steel molars, then pulled back. He pitched the head into the weeds, and a jolly football scrimmage ensued until the ball galloped away into a gully.

Tamara collapsed on the floor and clung to Filipp's leg. He covered his mouth with both hands. "Jesus Christ."

But one decapitation was enough, it seemed—a messy affair—for the remaining hostages were dispatched with bursts of automatic rifle fire to the back of the skull, as puffs of pink mist came from their faces.

"Allah the Almighty! Repeat this call, for it is a thunderbolt in the ears of the devils!"

Then from behind the camera a woman in black waddled out holding the bread-loaf form of a baby swaddled in a yellow blanket, and the narrator halted his litany to announce in plain Russian, "The seed of the terrorist state."

Tamara began screaming. Filipp dragged her from the room, but she fought him.

"Tamarochka!"

She clung, wailing, to the door frame as the tall mujahid shook the baby by the ankle and the swaddling tumbled free. The infant was swung back and forth (*one, two*) and then, before it was released into the heavens, Filipp shoved her to the entryway and pinned her to the wall.

In the other room, Kalashnikovs rattled.

"Allah the Most Supreme and the Most Almighty! Allah the Almighty! Allah the Almighty! Allah the Almighty!"

Then suddenly a woman's voice trilled from the television, and when Tamara again saw the set, an Indian in a sari was dancing and singing in falsetto—a Bollywood musical the killers of her son had taped over.

■ The day after Tamara saw the beggar child in the Vtoraya Rechka market, she visited the police station twice: at eight a.m. when it opened to the public, and after seven that evening when Lieutenant Yengalychev phoned and asked her to come down as soon as possible. When she arrived, he said her suspicions had been right. The woman had admitted the boy was a Russian kidnapped from Nalchik five years ago. The only thing she knew was that his name was Slava and both his parents were doctors.

"It's incredible," the lieutenant said. "I've never heard of such a thing in sixteen years of police work. Of course, the fingers must have tipped you off."

Then, pausing, he stood and busied himself at a tall filing cabinet with his back to her. After giving her a few minutes, he brought her a cup of mineral water. On his right hand he wore a wedding band.

"They kidnap children all the time," he said. "You can't blame yourself."

Tamara gulped the saline water. "Yes," she said. She had no interest in the policeman's absolution. "Where's my baby?"

"Just a minute. First there are a few matters we have to clear up. The captain wants a DNA test, but given the circumstances and her confession, we agreed we can send him home with you rather than put him in an orphanage while we await the results. You can have your photos back, but we've been asked to send the video to Moscow. Oh, and we've got some forms for you to fill out."

She began filling in the documents, streaking her cheek with the pen as she wiped her eyes. Lieutenant Yengalychev explained that the accused was a citizeness of the Chechen nationality, name of (he consulted his notes) Roza Damayeva, thirty-seven, widowed, lately an undocumented resident of Moscow, originally from Urus-Martan ("I've been there," he said. "It's a shithole"). She had confessed that the boy had indeed been kidnapped from his mother, but she insisted she wasn't the one who had grabbed Slava from his baby carriage. When the kidnapping occurred, Roza had been in Chechnya—so she claimed. Not like it mattered; the penalties for human trafficking were the same either way. The original kidnapper was an unknown female of Chechen descent, a heroin addict who happened to see an unattended baby in a carriage and walked off with it. A crime of opportunity. This woman sold the infant to a slaver, a Chechen named Makhmud Damayev, who was Roza's brother-in-law. Makhmud was some *sharia* judge, had actually studied in Jordan. He was the one who cut off the thumb and forefinger. But in the end, Makhmud gave the baby to Roza. Christ knows why. Probably because she was a widow and she could make use of him when she begged in the marketplace. A prop for sympathy. All they cared about was money, Chechens. Anyway, the perpetrators had sent the video to the Rudyakovs to cover their tracks. The baby murdered in the field that day—it was somebody else's.

"By the way," Lieutenant Yengalychev concluded, "Roza wants to talk to you. If you wish to, that is. Up to you."

"Yes. Yes, in fact, I'd like to hear what she has to say."

"I should warn you, she's looking rather, well, disheveled. It took a little persuasion to get her to talk." When Tamara stared at him, he asked, "Does that bother you?"

"Not in the least."

The lieutenant smiled.

They met Roza in an interrogation room where she sat on a stool, holding a torn flap of her blouse in place on her shoulder. Her face was bruised and swollen, and a bead of blood ballooned and deflated in her right nostril. On her scalp was a raw patch where her hair had been yanked out by the roots. Two of her teeth were missing and a third had been broken into a fang. All this Tamara observed ruthlessly as she humped her way into the room and sat in a chair with her crutches propped on her knee.

Roza stared at her, then lowered her eyes. "You're Dr. Rudyakova?"

"Yes."

"Did they tell you I didn't kidnap him?"

A nod.

"I never hurt him. It was my brother-in-law who cut off his fingers. Understand, I raised him like my own son."

It was all Tamara could do to refrain from yanking out another fistful of hair. When she spoke, she discovered she was out of breath. "But he wasn't. Wasn't your son."

"No." Belatedly, Roza noticed the crutches. "What's wrong with your legs?"

"The day you people sent us the videotape I stepped off the roof of our apartment. But fifteen stories isn't high enough, it seems—not if you're stupid enough to fall into a tree."

"Oi!" Roza wiped her nose, smearing blood. Then almost inaudibly she added, "I'm sorry."

"Did you know that my husband worked for the Red Cross and was risking his life to provide medical aid to Chechen civilians?"

Roza shook her head.

"So is that all you wanted to say?" Tamara asked. "That it wasn't your fault?"

"No, listen. When I first saw Az—saw the boy—, Makhmud (he's my brother-in-law), he was keeping him a prisoner in his basement in Urus-Martan. So I took the baby home and looked after him. He would have died otherwise, understand? And then once Makhmud got his share of the money, he decided—"

"Wait. What money?"

"Yours. The ransom."

"I thought Malofeyev ran off with it."

"Malofeyev and Makhmud were partners."

Tamara digested this.

"And so, after Makhmud gave me the baby, he sent you that video-tape so you'd think Slava was dead. Malofeyev didn't want any part of this; he said you'd paid and we should return the baby. He even threatened to go to the police, so Makhmud had him killed. They dangled a stick of dynamite on a rope outside the window of his apartment and had him blown up in his bed, along with his wife and daughter."

"So whose baby did you murder in the place of my son?"

"You don't understand, we didn't kill anyone. That was just a video they bought in the marketplace. I heard the baby was the daughter of a Russian officer. They snatched her at gunpoint from her mother's apartment in Buynaksk." As an afterthought, she added, by way of justification, "The man whose head they cut off, I heard he was a Jew."

"Jesus Christ."

"There's one more thing I want to tell you. What the Russians did to my sons."

"You want one on the snout, bitch?" Lieutenant Yengalychev slapped Roza's face, and blood flecked the floor two meters away. "Do you think anybody gives a shit about you?"

Tamara waited to see if the policeman would strike Roza again. When he did not, she exhaled. "All the same, I'd like to hear."

"Could I have a sip of water?" Roza said. "My throat."

"If you've got something to say, just say it," the lieutenant told her.

Roza swallowed. "In the summer of 1996 a Russian convoy was ambushed near our village, and so the following night the Russians came to our village and arrested all the men. Seized them from their beds, the ones who didn't manage to run off. They also took a teenage girl whom we never heard from again. When the soldiers kicked down our door, I told them there were no men in the house, my husband had died in a car accident years ago. So they took my sons instead. My boys were fourteen and sixteen years old. Just loaded them into a truck with all the men and drove off. For nine months I looked for my boys, visiting army bases and prison camps—places where they hold them in open pits under the rain and the snow—but I never found them. Then one day I got a message from a Russian sergeant offering to sell me my youngest for two hundred dollars: Azamat—he was named Azamat, too. So I borrowed from everyone I knew to buy his freedom. In exchange, they directed me to a place in the forest where they had dumped his corpse.

"From this moment, my hatred for Russians became a fever in me. I wanted to poison every Russian child, to cut off the breasts of every Russian mother. I wanted every woman from Kaliningrad to Anadyr to experience what I did, to bathe her son's corpse for his funeral, to touch the rope burns and ulcers from trench foot and the dislocated jaw and the bloody ridge where his left ear had been torn from his head. To wake every night hearing his screams in her dreams. And Slava, when I heard about him, I hated him, too. The child of the Russian murderers. Makhmud was keeping the baby in his dungeon, and another hostage—a Russian army private, a dark, frightened boy from Buryatia—was caring for Slava, cradling him under his coat.

"But Makhmud sold the private, and so Slava was alone except for a Russian grandfather who'd lost his mind after sitting in the dark for almost a year. One of Makhmud's daughters was feeding the baby a few times a day, but that was all. The rest of the time he cried; you could hear it as you passed by outside the building. One day, Makhmud took me down to look at the baby. He thought it would please me to see a Russian child suffering. But when the flashlight found him, Slava was lying in an open suitcase, naked in his own filth, with no one around but the old man, who was gibbering about demons. The baby started screaming when he heard Makhmud's voice. He looked like a handful of sticks in a bag of skin. The stubs of his finger and thumb were stained with *zelyonka*—

somebody had at least thought to disinfect the wounds. 'There it is, the glory of Russia: its youth,' Makhmud said. The poor little one. I couldn't help it, I picked him up and started singing to him, an old mountain song, and he stopped crying. So desperate for a human touch. Makhmud tried to grab the baby from me, and Slava's tiny fingers clung to my blouse. And although I knew nothing could ever erase my grief, this need of his planted a seed of hope inside me. Someone to care for."

"That's all lies," the lieutenant said. "I was in Chechnya, and nobody was arresting teenagers—only terrorists."

"Can't you get her some water?" Tamara asked. "She can barely speak."

Lieutenant Yengalychev found a paperclip in his pocket and cleaned his thumbnail with it. "Let her drink from the squatter when she gets back to her cell."

"So, let me see if I get this right," Tamara told Roza. "At the time Slava disappeared, the war was over, the Russian army had retreated, you had de facto independence for your shitty little republic, and you people still thought you were justified in kidnapping Russian babies because bad things had once happened to you? This is your point?"

Stated thus, the words demanded a denial, but to Tamara's surprise the woman nodded. Tears streamed down her cheeks. "I just wanted you to know that I love Azamat—love Slava. He's my son, too."

The lieutenant kicked the stool out from under Roza and sent her sprawling.

"Love? What do you know about love, you bitch? You people are a disgrace to Islam."

■ Tamara found the boy in an office that looked out through barred windows at the crowd waiting at the Magnitogorskaya bus stop. He sat at a table with a pencil and paper, drawing a tank that was shelling a kremlin. He watched her as she approached, his dirty face tear-streaked.

Tamara pulled up a seat beside him. "They told you?"

"Yes."

"Do you believe them—that I'm your mama?"

Slava shook his head: No, no, no, no, no.

She removed a small makeup mirror from her bag and leaned in close to him. "Look at us. Our eyes are the same, our hair. How could Roza be your mother?"

Slava stared as if frightened of what the mirror might reveal. Then he shook his head again. No. Never.

From her pocket she produced a tin soldier, a painted infantryman from the Preobrazhensky Regiment, Napoleonic Wars era. "I brought you a present."

"I don't want it."

"You asked me for a soldier."

"It's not the right kind. I wanted a mujahid."

"The mujahideen are terrorists and murderers. They stole you from your papa and me. Roza, too: maybe she acted kind, but she kept you from your real mama. We loved you, and they destroyed us. Your papa, too. You know he's alive? He lives in Moscow. We'll call him tonight."

Slava tore a corner off his page and then was unsure what to do with it. He started to slip it into his mouth. She took the scrap from his hand.

"Slava—you know your name is Slava?—when I last saw you, you were this big. Shorter than my forearm, poor little hare."

"I know."

Tamara gave the boy a sidelong hug. Slava did not know what to do and kept his hands on the table, smoothing the torn edge of his drawing. She kissed him, buried her face in his hair, savored the smell of her baby beneath the odors of mutton and Tajik tobacco smoke. The boy tried to pull away, but she held him. He began to sob against her breast. His tears and warm breath penetrated her summer blouse and her bra, and she remembered the sensation of nursing, strings and despair. Had it done him any good at all, those three weeks at her nipple? Yet as they sat there, she found an unexpected comfort in what Roza had told her: even in captivity, the boy had been loved. Few of the child hostages of Chechnya could say as much. She wondered if Slava could ever learn to love her. If not, who could blame him? Tamara was unworthy of love. After all, it was her sin that had sown the bitter field of tares that Slava would spend his life scything.

"It's time to go." She stood, holding the boy's maimed hand as she adjusted her crutches. When he did not move, she told him again, "Slava, it's time."